FALLING PREY

STELLA MACLEAN

Cataloguing and Publication information is available from The Canadian ISBN Service System, Library and Archives Canada.

Title: Falling Prey/Stella MacLean

Identifiers:

ISBN: Print: 978-1-7778199-7-2
Ebook: 978-1-7778199-8-9

Formatting Services: Sweet' N Spicy Designs
Cover Design: https://www.hellhagproductions.com

CHAPTER ONE

Emily Carling struggled to keep up with her daughter, her hand luggage bumping repeatedly against her leg. Her other hand laced through the strap of her purse, her boarding pass clutched in her fingers, she hurried along. "Grace, slow down."

"Sorry, Mom. But I'm a little rushed. I forgot about the road construction near the airport," Grace said over her shoulder. "I can't be late for court."

"I understand, dear. We're nearly at the gate," Emily said, spotting her gate number.

They slowed as they approached the check-in counter.

"Mom, I don't understand why you're determined to go to Newfoundland so soon. Just because a man asked you to go doesn't mean you have to, does it? No man is worth tossing your life over for him. Why don't you postpone the trip for a little longer? Why don't you tell him—?"

"Tell Gus what?" she interrupted, annoyed that she was once again having to explain her decision. "That my daughter doesn't want me to leave Boston? To start a new life with the man I love?" she asked.

"Mom, I don't understand why you feel you have to go there. I'm worried about you, about what could happen to you. It's dangerous, you travelling alone to another country. I know Canada is not that different from here, but Newfoundland is a long way away. I had to look it up on the map, for heaven's sake! Did you know it's on the edge of the North Atlantic?"

"Yes. And it's a wonderful place. Very scenic. Gus has told me all about it, sent me videos and everything. We have plans to travel all over Newfoundland and Labrador."

Grace sighed. "Why don't you wait until I can go with you?"

"But your court work's scheduled months ahead. I can hardly get you to plan a vacation, let alone come to Newfoundland with me."

"I realize that, but as I said before we could work something out. Maybe we both go for a long weekend. It's not too late to change your mind."

"Grace, I want someone in my life. And Gus and I have been emailing, talking on the phone, on Facetime, on Zoom for months now. I know more about him now than I knew about your father when I married him. Your father and I had only been dating three months when we got married. And that turned out just fine. We were happy together for forty years."

Grace nodded, an anxious look still evident on her face.

"Please don't worry, Grace. What Gus and I have is special. I wasn't going to tell you this because I didn't know what you'd think. But I feel about Gus the way I felt about your father when I met him."

"Seriously?"

"Maybe not exactly the same, but the feeling that he's the one, that this is meant to be." She took her daughter's hand, willing her to understand. "Gus and I have talked about everything. He and I know each other as much as anyone can know someone without spending time together."

"Mom, I know you're lonely. Ever since Dad died you've miss having someone in your life. But let's face it. You met this Gus Parsons on a dating site. You have no idea what he's really like."

"My relationship with Gus is more than that, and you know it. Gus has been super kind to me. He had one of those full-length TV screens installed at my house so we could talk on FaceTime and Zoom. All to make it easier for us to talk as if we were together. For heaven's sake Grace, you and I have had coffee with him on Zoom several times at my house. He sent a whole bunch of videos that show where he lives in the countryside and where his office is in downtown St. John's."

"I know that..." Grace pursed her lips, a sure sign that she was not done arguing. "I realize that you had all sorts of legal stuff to work where the company was concerned," referring to her parents' transport company. "All that on top of dealing with grief. You meet this man who seems perfect, but no one's perfect, Mom. I think you need to take it slow. That's all I'm saying."

Emily wished with all her heart that her daughter would understand. "Like you say, I've spent a lot of time getting all my affairs in order. And you've been a huge help. But I need more than playing bridge, looking after the garden and going to exercise classes for seniors. Is that all there is to life after sixty? Really?"

"No. Of course not."

"Then, trust me to know what I'm doing. I'm not going for good, at least not yet. I have an open return ticket." She glanced at her daughter, seeing the way her short cropped black hair framed her face, her elegant features, her statuesque appearance, a beautiful blend of her parents.

"Grace, I have to meet Gus. I have to know if we could be

happy together. I can't know that on FaceTime or Zoom. I need to live with him under the same roof, be part of his everyday life, see for sure if this is for me."

"But why do you have to leave the country to do it?"

"You've done it. Lived with a man. You're the one who told me that it was the only way to know for sure if he was right for you."

"I didn't leave the country to live with Jake. And he wasn't right for me, Mom. That's my point. I thought he was. We'd been dating right here in Boston. I knew his friends, his family and still things didn't work out. As much as I wanted that relationship to be the one for me, we had issues we couldn't resolve."

"I don't know of any issues between Gus and me."

Grace threw up her hands. "That's my point, Mom. You don't know enough about each other to have issues. It takes time and shared experiences to really know. Knowing him online for few months is not enough."

"Honey, I'm sixty-three. Not thirty-five like you. My life is slipping past me. I want to live. I want to love someone again. I got through losing your dad. And now I need more in my life than simply having lunch with friends, and going out to social events. Can you understand that? He loves me and I love him."

"And I love you, Mom. It's just that I don't have a good feeling about this. Why can't he come here to meet your friends and family and stay for a couple of months? Why do you have to be the one to go to his place where you don't know anyone?"

"I do know someone. My friend Millie Hanson went online a couple of months ago and met a man who lives in St. John's. We talked just a couple of weeks ago. She says she's very happy with him. I don't know many of the details, but

I'm sure when I get to St. John's she'll tell me all about him. I plan to see her, introduce her to Gus.

"Besides his consulting work needs him there. My business is well-managed. Your father saw to that. Gus has a daughter, Penny, and a granddaughter he doesn't want to be away from right now. Some sort of upset going on with his daughter's work. She's a single mom."

She heard her flight being called. Emily looked at her daughter, at the stress lines bracketing her mouth. She worked too hard and worried too much. "Grace, we've been over all this before. I don't want to argue with you anymore. My flight leaves soon. I have to go through security. I'll call you from Montreal and as soon as I land in St. John's." She gave her daughter a quick hug. "Look at it this way. If he turns out to be a dud, at least I will have seen a little bit of Canada. I've never been to Newfoundland."

Grace shrugged, rolled her eyes. "You're not going to change your mind, are you?" Grace hugged her mother tight before stepping back, anxiety clouding her expression. "You charged your cell phone, did you?"

"And I have my battery charger with me." Emily gave her daughter the thumbs up.

"I'm going to miss you, Mom."

"I'll miss you too."

"Love you," Grace said, her eyes shiny with tears.

Emily felt her throat tighten at the thought of leaving her daughter, her only child and her safety net in the three years since her husband passed away. "Ah, Gracie, I'll miss you, so much. But we'll be together soon."

Grace nodded before turning away, her shoulders straight as she strode down the corridor and out of sight.

.　.　.

Hours later, after making it through the airport in Montreal, Emily waited for her two suitcases to arrive at the luggage carousel in the St. John's airport.

She'd had a horrible experience at Canadian customs in Montreal. The customs agent, a woman, questioned her carefully about why she was going to Newfoundland, how long she was staying, did she know the people she was going to visit. The questions were so upsetting. As if that wasn't enough the woman gave her a lecture, or that's what it felt like, about the dangers of traveling alone to meet up with a man, a stranger. That women needed to be more careful.

People milling around her, hands waving, luggage carts clanging--all of it set her nerves on edge. The long flight and the horrible customs agent had given her more time to think about her daughter's words.

What if I'm wrong? What if coming to St. John's is the worst decision I've ever made?

She'd always relied on Mark, her husband, to look after their travel arrangements, and always felt perfectly safe wherever they'd gone, whatever country they'd visited. Now, she felt unsettled by all this. She sighed, her shoulders aching from pulling her tippy carryon.

She called her daughter when she arrived in Montreal and as soon as she landed in St. John's. During both calls, her daughter sounded upbeat, made her promise to call every day, and wished her well. She even said nice things about Gus.

Wonders never cease, Emily thought just as her name came over the loudspeaker. She was directed to a courtesy phone. Leaving her spot next to the carousel, she made her way to the phone--and saw Gus standing in front of it, a wide, smile on his face. After all the photos he'd sent, she knew him on sight. She ran to him, threw her arms around his neck and hugged him close.

"I'm so glad you're here safe and sound," he said, holding onto her, his hug strong and warm. "I was a few minutes late, and thought the easiest way to find you would be to page you. How was your flight?" he asked, letting go of her and slipping his hand into hers.

"Customs in Montreal was a bit of a drag, but other than that, just fine," she said, drawing in the scent of his expensive cologne, seeing the look of appreciation and pleasure on his face. "I'm glad to be here," she murmured, leaning closer to him.

"Not as glad as I am, let me tell you." He put his arm around her and guided her back to the luggage carousel. "Let's get your bags and get out of here. I've got dinner organized. As you know, I only live about half an hour from here. It's a little foggy tonight, but we'll be fine."

He picked up the bags she pointed out, swung them onto a luggage cart, all without letting go of her hand. She loved that he wanted to keep her close, touch her. But she shouldn't be surprised. Gus had made it clear that he was what he called "touchy-feely." She hadn't known how much she missed being touched until he'd taken her hand in his. The need to touch was something they shared, something she was looking forward to experiencing over the next few weeks.

"God. I'm glad you're here," he said, as he led the way out of the airport arrivals area. "I can't believe we're finally going to be together. And like I said, you can sleep wherever you want. I had my housekeeper make up one of the spare bedrooms for you. It has its own bath, and outside it, there's a sitting area where you can read. I know how much you love to read. But what's most important here is I want you to do whatever suits you. There's no pressure. This is the perfect chance for us to get to know one another."

She held his hand with both of hers. "You can't imagine how I've waited for this day."

Out in the parking lot he led her to the passenger door of his Cadillac SUV. He opened it and helped her inside. Minutes later, with the luggage stowed in the back, he got into the driver's seat. With a big sigh he looked at her and smiled. "This feels so right. *We* feel right, don't we?"

"We do. It's wonderful for me to feel like this again," she said, taking in his face, the gentle smile, the look in his eyes.

"We can have it all, you and me. And we're only getting started," he said, turning to her, taking her hands in his. "Did you call Grace and let her know you got here safely?"

"Yes. She seemed pleased."

He didn't start the car right away. "Look, Emily, I can understand your daughter's concern about you traveling alone. You'll never know how much I appreciate your willingness to come here when I couldn't go to Boston, but I don't want to miss out on any more of our life together. And we will be together." He reached into his jacket pocket and brought out a small box wrapped in silver paper and passed it to her. "This is just a little something I picked up from a jeweler here in St. John's. They reminded me of you."

She took the box, slipping the wrapping off and opened it. Inside, nestled in burgundy velvet, was a pair of pendant earrings with a circle of filigreed gold suspended on each. "They're beautiful," she said, touching them. She looked into his smiling face and knew she'd made the right decision. She took her tiny gold studs out of her ears and placed them in a zipped area of her purse. "I'm going to wear them."

"Here, let me," he said, taking the box, lifting them out one at a time while she put them on.

Pulling the rearview mirror toward her, she turned her head from side to side, the gold glinting in the interior cabin light. "They're really lovely."

"Eighteen carat gold," he said proudly.

"They'll remind me of you every time I wear them," she

said. She saw the way he was looking at her, his eyes on her mouth. She leaned in. His hand slid to the nape of her neck.

"This is the happiest I've been for a long time," he said, easing his lips to hers, his scent surrounding her, his maleness flooding her senses. It had been so long since any man had kissed her. She reached her hands up to his throat, her fingers working under the edge of his shirt collar, the warmth of his skin inviting.

He kissed her again, followed by a deep shuddering breath. "We'll never get out of this parking lot if we keep this up," he said, a smile on his face as he pulled back and looked into her
eyes.

"You're right. And you must be starving after waiting for my flight to arrive," she said, feeling young and carefree, without a thought about food.

"We are just a pair of crazy teenagers," he said, leaning back in his seat as he started the car.

The radio came on, the announcer reporting foggy conditions and warning about limited visibility around the city. He announced that there would be a violinist from the Toronto Symphony Orchestra performing with a local ensemble from Memorial University early the next month.

"Would you like to go to that performance? I can get us tickets, if you'd like to."

"That's sweet of you. Yes, let's plan to go."

"Consider it done," he said, concentrating on the road ahead.

In the quiet of the car with only a whisper of sound coming from the powerful engine, the soft light of the console reflecting on his face, she knew with certainty that this man would care for her, be kind to her. "I'm excited about seeing your house, and meeting Jasmine," she added.

"You'll love her. She's the best little dog, so companionable. We'll have lots of lovely walks with her," he said as he waited at the stoplight.

"It's been a long time since I walked a dog," she said wistfully, lulled by the rhythmic sounds of traffic passing, and the undulating brightness from the light poles along the side of the road.

"I've got a standing rib roast in the oven. It should be done in about a half hour," he said, glancing across at her. "And your favorite, apple pie."

"That sounds delicious."

"And I bought a bottle of Krug to celebrate our first meeting because you love champagne. I know it's not our first meeting, in a way, but having you here with me, being able to touch you... It's all I want."

"Me too. When I first went on that dating site, I was really not sure it was a good idea. And the men...either weird or so set in their ways... Sorry. I told you all that before. But then you contacted me. I'm so glad you did," she said, feeling perfectly at ease.

CHAPTER TWO

E mily settled deeper into the plush seat, peering out at the headlights jabbing the fog. She had no idea where they were, but it didn't really matter. She was with Gus. "I grew up in Boston and I've never seen fog like this before," she said, glancing over at him, his profile strong, his hands on the wheel so reassuring.

"If I could have picked today's weather, it would've been a balmy, bright day, not this pea soup," he said.

She heard an undercurrent of exasperation in his voice. Wanting to please him, she murmured, "It's okay. You told me to expect foggy weather sometimes."

She didn't want him to be upset. She wanted him to be as excited as she was, excited and eager for this new adventure. She wanted them to be together the way they'd talked about during all their conversations.

She really didn't mind the fog. Yet, as she stared out the window at the billowing waves of gray rushing past the windshield, she wondered how he'd know where his driveway was when they reached it.

As if reading her mind, he said, "I have lights embedded in

the mailbox at the end of my driveway to allow me to see where to turn. When I first moved into the house I had to change a few things, including marking the driveway so I wouldn't miss it. I got lost one day in the fog and ended up getting a police escort back to the house. Very embarrassing. But the officer, Greg Neilson, became a friend. It doesn't hurt to have a friend on the police force. We had him and his wife to dinner before Annabelle became so ill. He often drops by when he's out this way."

As if by magic a bright yellow light appeared, and Gus slowed the vehicle, turned into the driveway and accelerated gently. "We're almost home," he said, a smile lighting his face.

"That's great," she said, aware of large trees sweeping past the car and what looked like flowerbeds sketched out at their base in the murky fog.

Gravel crunched under the tires. Headlights dipped and swayed. A stone wall appeared out of the grayness. She looked again. Not a stone wall, the wall of a house with tiny lights trying valiantly to illuminate the darkness. Gus touched a button on the visor, turned the car and suddenly a large garage door opened up. He eased into the space, the purr of the vehicle becoming a soft roar, reverberating off the walls.

"We're here," he said, shutting off the engine, turning to her, pulling her into his embrace and kissing her. A demanding kiss that left her tingling.

Surprised, but happy, she returned his kiss. "I can't wait to meet your daughter Penny, and your granddaughter Tessa. It will be fun getting to know them, especially getting to know Tessa. I haven't had a four-year-old to spoil since Grace was that age. Will we see them tomorrow?"

"We need a couple of days to ourselves. You need to unpack, get used to the house, and have a leisurely walk around the property. You'll meet my daughter and grand-daughter very soon."

"Maybe we can all go on Zoom together."

"Maybe, but first let's spend some time together, see how we make out. Like we said on Zoom a few weeks ago, learning to live together is going to be a big change for both of us. Then, we'll have Tessa and Penny over to dinner."

"I'd like that." She sighed. "Oh, by the way, I took your advice about shipping a few things over to your house. They should be here in a couple of weeks."

"That's great. It makes me feel like we're making progress on starting our new life together. And having a few of your things here will make you feel more at home. Like I said to you, it's about being a couple, making our own decisions. We need to start creating our own memories. This is our time, and I don't want to miss a minute of it. Having a few of your things will make my home feel like yours, don't you think?"

"I do. And like you said, there's no reason to tell Grace. She has her own life. And we have our new life together here."

"Yeah, I think you and I decided that you'd ship a desk, your antique blanket box and a couple of other things," he said. He opened the door, went to the back and got her luggage out before she had time to get out of the car.

He is both eager and gallant, she mused. Since her husband Mark had died, she'd grown accustomed to taking her own luggage wherever she went. Such a refreshing change.

Putting the suitcases down, he pressed his thumbprint onto a screen near the back door. With a whirring sound the door eased open. "I told you about my security system, didn't I?" he asked, probably because of the surprise that must have shown on her face. At home, she had a simple deadbolt and a security code that only her neighbor, her daughter and her cleaning lady knew.

"Yes, you told me," she said, as she followed him into the house, into what was clearly a utility area with a bathroom off to one side, a closet on the other side, and a short corridor leading to the rest of the house. She hadn't seen this part of the house when he sent all those videos weeks ago.

"I'm going to take your bags up to the guest room. I'll be back in a few minutes."

She followed him into the kitchen, a space she recognized from the videos. She put her purse on the black-and-white marble counter and walked around the kitchen. It was even more beautiful than she imagined with the white French colonial cabinets, the silvered backsplash and pewter handles on all the cupboards. The stove was a huge propane one. It looked different from her electric one, but she'd enjoy learning to use it all the same. The wine fridge under the drinks area was backlit showing more bottles of wine and champagne than she'd had ever seen, except in a specialty liquor store. One of the wall ovens was whirring, it's interior light on, reminding her that he'd set the oven before he picked her up at the airport.

There were black stools lined up along the outside edge of the cooking island. She climbed onto one of them and continued looking around. She didn't want to get ahead of herself, but if things worked out and this became her home… The thought excited and frightened her at the same time.

She was still looking around when Gus came into the kitchen. "What do you think?"

"It's gorgeous. I've never seen a kitchen like this. Mark and I were pretty basic in our living arrangements. In the early years of getting his cargo business going, we put the money into the business. Then later, we bought a summer home and traveled a lot."

"When I first moved to Newfoundland and met Annabelle, she and I thought we might build a new home together. But she loved it here, and I really didn't care where I lived as long as I was with her." He took the champagne from the wine fridge. "This house was about half the size when I moved in. But by the time Annabelle and I were finished renovating, we had every modern convenience we could think of installed in the kitchen. And of course, being in the security business, I had it outfitted with the latest technology."

"Amazing. I've got a lot to get used to," she said, as a thumping sound filled the air.

"Whoops! I forgot about Jasmine," he said, going to a door along the far wall. A beautiful King Charles Spaniel pattered toward Emily.

"Oh, I am so glad to meet you, Jasmine," she said, kneeling down and opening her arms. The dog rushed in, licked her face, her tail wagging as she cuddled close. "I miss Freddy, our King Charles. But he was an old dog, and I think he died of a broken heart after Mark passed away." She hugged the wiggling dog close, feeling its warmth against her skin. "You and I are going to go for long walks, aren't we?"

A cork popped. Jasmine stopped wiggling, snuffling Emily's hand.

"Time for bubbly," Gus said, taking two champagne flutes out of the massive fridge.

Emily eased back onto her stool, noting that the dog sat down near her. She and Jasmine would get along just fine, and she would have a dog in her life again.

"The roast smells delicious," she said, feeling more upbeat than she'd felt in months; no, make that years. For the three years since Mark died.

The sound of champagne quietly gurgling, as it pooled in the flute while Gus poured, put her in a festive mood. "I think we should toast our future," she said, as she took the glass from his fingers.

"I want to toast to a new beginning, to a new life for both of us." He leaned in, kissed her and smiled. "We are going to have a wonderful life together. No worries, just lots of fun and travel, quiet evenings by the fire, and good food. To us," he said, touching his flute to hers.

"To us," she replied, her heart full, excitement welling up in her. "We're the luckiest two people on the planet."

The next morning Emily awoke to bright sunshine pouring in through the broad expanse of casement windows in her bedroom. After the delicious dinner with wine after the champagne, she'd found herself too sleepy to stay awake. Gus had been caring and concerned about her sudden lag in energy, and had taken her up to her bedroom, a massive space with a large bathroom. She hadn't unpacked anything last night, and now faced the two suitcases stacked on the luggage rack at the foot of her bed.

She checked her watch. Nearly eight. *Where is Gus? Should I go and find him, tell him I'm taking Jasmine for a walk after I unpack? Or is he downstairs making breakfast, in which case I'll join him as soon as I get dressed.*

Their first breakfast together.

She opened the bedroom door. There was a sheet of paper on the floor. In big block letters were the words: *In my office working. Urgent situation at work. Fresh coffee in carafe. Help yourself to croissants. See you about eleven. Love, Gus.*

She heard the patter of Jasmine's paws on the shiny wooden floor. "Are you looking for a walk?" she asked, giving the dog's back a good rub. Jasmine wagged her tail and looked up at Emily with huge brown eyes.

"You are, aren't you? I'll get dressed and take you out," she said, as the dog followed her back into the bedroom. Despite being exhausted after dinner she did remember Gus showing her the door that led to the garden and to the pathways around the property. She'd go out into the garden with Jasmine and find a comfy spot to call Grace.

After pulling on jeans and a turtleneck sweater she came back downstairs. She found her jacket right where Gus said it would be, in the closet near the door that led to the garden. There was a dog leash hanging on the wall. She clipped it on Jasmine, tucking her phone into her pocket as she opened the door. A muted beeping sound erupted, reminding her of his elaborate security system. It would take a little getting used to, but she'd manage.

Outside, she called Grace's number and waited for her to pick up. Instead she got a beeping sound she didn't recognize. Maybe the phone system here in Newfoundland was different than back home in Boston. She'd try again later on her walk.

Stepping out into the sunny garden with the scent of daylilies wafting around her, Emily drew in a deep breath and raised her face to the sun. The warmth was relaxing, and the cheerful chirp of chickadees uplifting. It was going to be a lovely day.

She pulled gently on the leash and she and Jasmine started down the long driveway, the trees folding overhead as they walked. Jasmine frolicked along the gravel drive, turning suddenly onto a narrow pathway that led into the trees. "You know this route, do you?" Emily asked, following the dog.

Once on the path, the trees came closer together, at times forcing Emily to hold back branches so that she could pass. Then, suddenly they were out in an open space in what seemed to be a garden with a wooden structure that looked like a tool shed and a trellis with climbing roses. There were

17

shrubs everywhere and a bench along one side of the walkway. She'd sit down and call Grace while she enjoyed the space.

Grace answered on the first ring. "Hi Mom, I'm in the car on my way to work. How are you doing?"

"I'm doing just great, dear. Gus's home is beautiful. Jasmine is a wonderful dog. I'm out for a walk with her right now, and we found a bench in one of the gardens on the property. We had champagne last evening and Gus made dinner. He gave me a beautiful pair of gold earrings." She sighed at the memory. "How are you doing?"

"Better, now that I've heard from you. What are your plans for today?"

"Gus had to go to work in his home office, and I don't know what we'll be doing once his meeting is over; some sort of situation at work. But I'm sure we'll do something fun later. I've never been to St. John's, and I'm looking forward to that. What's on for you today?"

"I'm on my way to court. Another divorce hearing. The usual stuff."

"I wish you practiced a less stressful form of law. I worry that you're going to get caught up in some sordid case of domestic violence."

"Mom, it's my job. I'm used to it. Besides, right now my only real relationship is with our private investigator, Hank Snow."

"Every time you say his name I think of the country singer from Nova Scotia, Hank Snow."

"No comparison Mom. My Hank is a dapper dresser, very cosmopolitan and has a bevy of women waiting for his call. Wish I could say the same for me – a bevy of men in my case."

"Someday maybe I'll get to meet Hank. I tried to call you earlier, but the call didn't go through."

"Why not?"

"Have no idea. But Gus's house is up a very long lane away from the highway, and the highway leading here is off another highway. I really have no idea where I am, which will mean I'll have to drive with Gus until I figure it out. He's got a second car I can use. He says it's mine for as long as I want."

"Seriously, Mom? You have no idea where you are?"

"Well...I know it's a very exclusive area outside St. John's. The houses are all back off the road, and he has a very elaborate security system on the house. To be expected I guess given that he once ran a high-tech security company."

"I guess so. Have you met Penny yet?"

"Not yet, but I just got here. So much new to get used to, but it's been great so far. I'm going to see if Gus would like to have her and her daughter to dinner some evening this week. It would be nice to get to know her."

"She wasn't in on any of the Zoom calls or the FaceTime you had with him?"

"No. She lives somewhere in St. John's."

"Oh! Mom, I've got another call and I'm nearly at the courthouse. Talk to you tomorrow."

"Yes. Love you."

"You too."

Putting the phone back in her pocket, she let her eyes follow the path. From where she sat she could see a small statue nestled against a yew tree. "Let's see what that's about," she said to Jasmine as she started along the path. The statue was of a woman holding a leash, as if she had a dog. Funny... Moving closer, she saw that the leash was made to look like real rope...interesting...and through the loop of the rope something glinted...

"Emily!" Gus called.

"I'm here, Gus. In the garden near the driveway," she said

as he burst through the branches along the path, a look of concern on his face.

"This is so beautiful. Like a secret garden," she said, coming toward him.

His smile warmed her. "It is a secret garden. It was Annabelle's passion. She loved growing things. I haven't done much with it since she passed; too many memories." He took her hand, his fingers warm on hers. "How was your walk? Did you go up or down the road?"

"Neither. I was walking Jasmine down the driveway when she veered off onto this path. It's such a lovely place. I'd love to look after it. My flowerbeds in Boston were all looked after by gardeners, but before we had the money I did all of it myself."

"You can do whatever you like with this garden. The rest of the grounds are cared for by a landscaping company. In the meantime, I've started breakfast for us." He leaned down and kissed her. "And I'm really sorry I got caught in an early meeting this morning. How did you sleep?"

"Like the dead," she said, happy to have Gus beside her. "The moment my head hit the pillow I was gone."

"Well, after breakfast I'm going to take you on a walk around the property, show you all the gardens, the dog kennels that Annabelle had built. Did I tell you that she and her first husband bred Bernese Mountain Dogs?"

"No, you didn't. She must have been a pretty special woman from the way you describe her." Emily glanced at Gus, seeing a strange glint in his eyes. What was he thinking? Was he remembering his life with Annabelle? Missing her, maybe?

"Annabelle was special. As I told you, I met Annabelle after I moved here. I'd wanted a fresh start and bought an electronics business in St. John's. All good because I wanted to get away from Ontario where I'd lived. Penny was married and living in Ontario at the time, and I felt it was a good opportunity to give her a little space. But that didn't go as planned. She moved here right after she divorced her husband."

"I'm really anxious to meet Penny," Emily said as they walked together up to the house.

"She's in the midst of her biggest real estate deal since she moved here. In the meantime, I'll give you a quick tour of the property. Then we'll have breakfast. We'll go into St. John's later and I'll give you a tour. You'll love the city. Lots of history and local color."

"I'm looking forward to it, all of it," Emily said, taking his hand in hers.

They went around to the back of the house and he showed Emily all the garden spaces there. Emily was impressed that he knew many of the plant names.

"I want you to be happy here," he said, smiling at her, his hand brushing her shoulder, as she gazed up at him.

Emily smiled. "There is so much I'm looking forward to doing with you, and this property is lovely. Grace asked me where I am. Sounds like a silly question, but I have no idea. I think we took two roads to get here to your driveway, but I'm not sure."

"We're just a few miles outside St. John's. This area is mostly made up of homes and a couple of schools. There's no industry in this area, but there's a small port and a ferry that goes to Bell Island."

"I'm going to google it and see if I can get my bearings."

"Better still, on our way into St. John's I'll take you around to where the ferry docks."

"So, it's not that far from here?"

"On a different road, pretty country, lovely coastline. People here are very proud of their small villages and coastal communities, and many of them are tourist destinations." He led her into the house and through to the kitchen. "And we get a lot of tourists."

"But not here where you live."

"No. This is a very private area," he said as they entered the kitchen together.

"Oh, by the way, Gus, I don't know how to set or cancel the alarm on your system. I know you opened the door last night with your thumbprint, but unless I do something like that, how will I be able to get in the house if the system's on?"

"Oh. Yes. Forgive me. There will certainly be times when you want to leave the house, or come back in when I'm not here. What I'll do is give you the code, but let's leave it at that for now."

He led the way to the kitchen, taking a frying pan off the rack near the stove. "Why don't you keep me company while I make breakfast? Local sausages and eggs with toasted sourdough bread."

"You spoil me. You really do."

"I plan to look after you really well," he assured her as he poured coffee for both of them. "There's nothing I wouldn't do to protect you and look after you, Emily. I promise."

There was that strange glint in his eyes again.

CHAPTER THREE

Over the next day, Emily organized her new life with Gus. Being in his home was exciting and interesting. The rooms were tastefully decorated, the furniture exquisite, the art modern. It reminded her that she had a few pieces of furniture being shipped over to make her feel more at home here. She'd changed a few things in the kitchen to make it easier for her, more familiar. She'd begun opening all the blinds and drapes to let more light in to the rooms, especially the living room. She found the spaces gloomy whenever it was overcast outside.

She planned to change a few of the sofas around in the living room and library to take in the spectacular view of the forest behind the house. Gus had said she could add or change anything she wanted, and she took him at his word.

The bedroom she slept in faced the back garden with a view of deep green spruce and fir trees along the back of the space. She wanted to learn all about Gus's choices in art and furnishings, because he'd talked a lot about his home one night when they were on Zoom.

When she and Mark could afford to renovate their home

in Boston, they'd hired an interior design firm that made most of the decisions. She'd been too intimidated by the interior designer assigned to their project to question why he made the choices he did, but in the end her home was the envy of her friends.

Yet, seeing the eclectic choices in Gus's home she wanted to know more about how he chose the furnishing and art, or whether it was both he and Annabelle involved in the choices.

Speaking of Gus... He seemed to have a lot of business-related things to do in his office.

In a way Gus reminded her of Mark, whose business interests had taken a lot of his time. Though she'd always been welcome in Mark's office, she sensed that Gus didn't want her to come down to his office in the basement. It wasn't anything he said, only that he would suddenly say he had to go downstairs and he'd be down there until she called to him from the top of the stairs.

A really minor thing compared to all the nice things he'd done for her since she arrived. The earrings. The champagne. The tour of St. John's and lunch at La Soleil, a marvelous French Bistro in the old part of the city. They'd strolled along the streets after lunch, narrow steep streets bordered by colorful buildings and houses. She loved the façades of many old buildings, some of them dating back to the 1800s and earlier.

St. John's was known to have one of the best deep-water ports in the North Atlantic and when she toured the port area with Gus she could see why. Deep, cold water embraced by steep walls of stone that protected it from the ocean beyond. She'd asked him about going to Cape Race, where the first distress messages came in from the *TITANIC*, but he didn't seem interested. She planned to use Google maps and go there one day soon. Maybe Penny would go with her.

But today she planned to make a special dinner for them. The cleaning lady, Theresa McLaughlan – a lovely woman – had arrived and was upstairs working. The house would be clean and tidy for this evening. She found delicate Spode china in the china cabinet and would use it for this evening's meal. She wanted to do nice things for Gus. She'd forgotten to mention her problem with her cell phone, but she'd ask him that night.

Jasmine needed a walk, and Emily would take her down to the secret garden, a chance to look at the plants and shrubs again, and identify which ones were growing well and which weren't. She sighed with contentment.

The moment she took the leash from the hook at the back door, Jasmine ambled down the hall toward her. "We're going to get a little exercise, you and I," she said, managing to get the leash hooked on the dog's collar despite Jasmine's romping and twisting.

Once outside, they were only minutes getting to the garden. This time Emily brushed the branches away with ease and they were suddenly standing in the same spot they'd been in just a day ago. Today the air had a chill to it, and there were wisps of fog wafting along the tops of the trees. She suddenly felt uneasy.

Jasmine led the way toward the statue surrounded by bunchberry plants displaying their white flowers. She hadn't noticed those blooms the other day, but today she took note. Such a pretty sight, especially the mountain ash weighed down by clusters of orange-red berries that stood just beyond the statue. Striking. She knelt down to take a closer look at the statue, particularly the rope made of stone, its twisted shape so realistic. Through the rope, a few feet beyond the statue, something glinted despite the overcast day. "What do you suppose that is?" she said out loud.

Jasmine's ears perked up. "Should we have a look?"

The dog turned and pulled Emily along as it darted toward a clear spot in the bunchberries to the side of the statue. "Okay, we'll go there," she said, making for the spot. Once close to it, she saw a very narrow path covered with some sort of moss or lichen. She bent down to take a better look, the dog moving ahead of her over the ground.

Suddenly Jasmine gave a high-pitched bark, straining on the leash. "What is it?" Emily asked, scrambling to keep up with the dog.

Once out in the open, she stared. There were three small headstones fanned out in a half circle with moss and lichen growing between them. As she looked closer the clumps of moss seemed to be uneven as if they'd been moved recently. And the grass looked like rodents had lifted it, leaving a feeling that someone had disturbed this part of the garden.

Was it a graveyard? The back of her neck tingled at her uneasiness. She cautiously moved to the first headstone on the left. *Samuel.*

She moved to stand between the other two. *Sergeant. Sadie.*

What's this all about? Why are graves here in this spot? What do they mean?

Jasmine wiggled and leaped, pawing at Emily's leg. "It's okay, girl. We'll go back to the house now," she said, turning back toward the path through the trees, her steps hurried, her breath short. As she quickly headed for the house, all thoughts of taking Jasmine for a long walk evaporated into the cool morning air.

She reached the safety of the back door before looking over her shoulder. Thankfully she couldn't see the driveway or the path and certainly not the garden or the graves. *What was with those? Who is buried there?* She shivered.

Entering the house, she hurried into the kitchen, nearly knocking Theresa over. "Sorry!"

"Are you okay?" Theresa asked, putting her bucket down, the water sloshing.

"I...I just came from the...ah...cemetery?"

"Oh, you mean the pet cemetery? Down by Annabelle's garden?"

"Is that what it is?"

"Yes. Annabelle, and her first husband, bred Bernese Mountain Dogs. There are three headstones, but there are other dogs buried there. And I think a couple of cats. You weren't frightened by it, were you?" Theresa placed her mop in the bucket, stirring it in the soapy liquid.

"Tell me more about Annabelle," Emily said, unclipping Jasmine's leash and slipping out of her jacket.

"Annabelle and Elias Cleghorn were lovely people. They built this house, their dream house. She was an editor for some fancy literary journal and he was a retired Air Canada pilot. They were very happy until he died suddenly of a heart attack." Theresa propped her mop against the wall. "Annabelle grieved for months, was inconsolable until Gus came along. They got married and a few months later she became very ill. Her heart, I think. At first, I didn't really like Gus very much. There was something about him. But when Annabelle got sicker, he took over all her care. Stayed by her side. He asked me not to come the last few weeks.

"He wanted to do everything for her. It was awful when she died because he was out running errands and came home to find she'd passed away. I remember him telling me about it. He insisted that I come to work again, as if he didn't want to be alone here. He blamed himself for not being with her when she died. But those things happen, don't they?"

"That sounds like the Gus I know; caring and loving."

Theresa looked her up and down. "I hope you're going to be good for him. I want him to be happy. He's been a lost soul. He threw himself into his work at the women's shelter in town." Theresa rested her hands on her hips, her expression sad.

"Gus started to date women just months after Annabelle died. He was lonely I guess. There were three women in a row. I never met any of them, only knew about them because he'd mention them, seemed enthusiastic about them, and then suddenly he didn't talk about them anymore. I think he was trying to find someone just like Annabelle." Theresa shook her head. "That woman was one in a million."

"It must have been hard for him to adjust. It was hard for me when my husband died."

"I'm sorry for your loss. How did you meet Gus, if you don't mind my asking?"

"We met online."

"Really? I had a friend try that. She met a couple of guys from Saint Anthony, but they weren't what she was looking for. She did meet someone really nice at a bar one night, but he turned out to be married."

"I have a friend who met someone online. She moved here to be with him."

"Oh. Where?"

"I'm not sure. I think they live here in St. John's. Her name is Millie Hanson. I have her email address and cell phone number. I plan to get in touch with her once things settle down here."

"I was really pleased to see that Gus got a dog. Mind you, it's not the big dog like the Bernese dogs that Annabelle and her husband had, but it's sweet all the same."

"I love the King Charles Spaniel. My husband and I had one for years. Such good company." She reached down and rubbed the dog's ears. Jasmine licked her hand. "Jasmine is helping me get used to life here in Newfoundland."

"I suppose it's different than Boston."

"It is. Feels really strange to be living on an island. I know it's a huge island, but you can't leave here without getting on a plane or a boat. I'm not used to that. Living in Boston, I can go anywhere I want."

"You'll find the people here are very kind. And once you're settled you'll meet a lot of people. Gus has a lot of business friends, and of course he's devoted to his work at the women's shelter."

"I'm hoping to find a charity I can work with here. Or maybe take a few university courses. I'm working on a degree in European history, an interest of mine for years."

"Have you met Penny? Or Tessa?"

"No. I'm looking forward to it. But Gus says Penny's been really busy with her real estate job. Being a single parent is pretty difficult."

"Well, she's a different case, let me tell you. The first few times I met her, I wondered if she and Gus were even related – she was incredibly rude. When she moved here from Ontario, she seemed okay, but as time went on... And she was really difficult with Annabelle, but Annabelle got it straightened out."

"Oh?"

"Yes. Annabelle told Gus that if Penny didn't change her attitude, she didn't want her around. They had a big fight over it, just the week before Annabelle died in fact."

"Did Gus tell you that?"

"No. I heard it from my sister Mabel's son who works for the telephone company. He was in the house installing new cables or something and he heard the fight."

"Sometimes life can be pretty difficult," Emily said, not wanting to hear any more about Gus's life before she became part of it. He'd never talked very much about Annabelle, and she didn't think he'd want her finding things out her from the cleaning lady. Yet, there was one thing she was curious about. "Did Annabelle have family here?"

"No. She and Elias moved here from Vancouver when she got a job with the university. They didn't have any children, and no family living handy. But they didn't need anyone else. Oh, you should have seen them together... Absolutely devoted to each other."

When Gus got home later that day, Emily was in the living room reading a book she'd found on the bookshelf in her bedroom. It was the story of the Beothuk people who had inhabited parts of Newfoundland before the European settlers arrived. A very sad story, one that made her a little depressed. When she heard Gus's car coming up the driveway, she rushed to the back door, wanting to shake off the sadness.

"How was your meeting at the women's shelter?"

"The usual," he said, shrugging out of his coat. He looked so handsome with his hair messed a little, color in his cheeks and his navy-blue cashmere scarf draped around his neck. "It's chilly out there today."

She took his arm, leading him to the kitchen. "I know. I was out with Jasmine earlier today." She went to the liquor cabinet, planning to pour him an ounce of Macallan Scotch, neat, before she mixed her gin and tonic.

"Wait. I'll do that." He stepped around her and deftly prepared the drinks. "How was your day?"

"I found the pet cemetery. I mean I went for a walk with Jasmine. We were down by that statue and I saw a little path leading off."

"You weren't upset, were you?" he asked, passing her drink to her.

"No. Well, for a minute, yes. I didn't know what it was at first. But Theresa filled me in. The Gleghorns were really committed to their Bernese dogs, weren't they? I've never known of anyone who had a pet cemetery. I mean, have you?"

Gus clutched his scotch glass in his hand. "I...I helped Annabelle with that garden for the dogs. Sadie, her last Bernese dog, was the most wonderful animal you could ever imagine. She was devoted to us. She went everywhere in the car with us. We loved her," he said, his voice breaking.

"Oh! Gus, I'm sorry. I didn't mean to remind you of all that sadness."

"No. It's okay. We loved Sadie very much. She'd been the last bitch Annabelle and her husband had bred. Beautiful pups that everyone wanted." He sat down hard on the sofa, his head hanging down. "That's why I got Jasmine. I couldn't face getting a Bernese Mountain dog, too many memories, but Jasmine captured my heart."

Emily sat down beside him, taking his hand. "I know how it feels to love a pet. To want them to live forever. I really do. And I think creating that pet cemetery is really wonderful. And I'm sorry I brought it up."

"Don't be sorry. I would have told you about it. But not right away."

There was that glint in his eyes, his mouth twisted down. He looked so sad. "Oh, Gus, please. Let's enjoy our drinks and then we can think about dinner. I found some really lovely lamb chops in the freezer and have them thawing in the sink, maybe a few vegetables and salad. What do you think?"

"It all sounds perfect," he said, giving her a wan smile, the look in his eyes a little unsettling.

As Emily moved closer to him, she searched her mind for something that would pull him away from his memories about Annabelle and Sadie. She couldn't bear to watch him in pain and not be able to help. "What would you think if I found new plants for that area to brighten up the space? It is truly lovely, and it means a lot to you," she said, watching his face for his reaction.

He reached over, took her hand in his, and kissed her fingers, such a heady sensation. "You know what we might do?"

"What?" she asked, his smile lifting her spirits.

"Why don't we make a plan to get a new bench for the garden? There are several shops in St. John's that sell lawn ornaments and benches. Annabelle got the statue from one of them."

"What does the statue represent?" she asked, happy to see him feeling better.

"It's the statue from the movie *Midnight in the Garden of Good and Evil.* The rope part was added in memory of the dogs. Annabelle loved that movie, and was lucky enough to locate the statue."

"Then, we'll find a bench and I'll plant more flowers around the pathways. Did she have a plan for the garden? Maybe something she drew up?"

"I think there was one... Let me think. Yes, there was. It's down in my office. Come with me," he said, pulling her up with him.

Delighted to be getting to see his man cave – as she'd begun to think of it – she followed him down the narrow stairs to the basement level and into his office.

She stopped in the doorway, took in a deep breath, her eyes attracted to the array of computer screens surrounding his desk.

"I've never seen anything like this," she said, making her way into the room, her eyes still on the screens.

"It was originally part of my business, back before I sold. Now, I use it to stay in touch with people, the stock market, and of course it allows me to monitor my home alarm system and follow news broadcasts. Four screens all directed at different things. It's very common in my line of work," he said, moving past her to sit in the chair at his desk.

He clicked the mouse a couple of times and she saw a street view at the entrance to the property.

"So you can see whoever is coming up the driveway?"

"Of course. I have motion detectors that trigger lights to come on, and cameras to record any activity. See this," he said, pointing to the screen that showed her walking with Jasmine. "When you left the house, you triggered the camera to record your movements."

"That feels a little spooky," she said, mesmerized by what she saw.

"It shouldn't be. It's simply being safe and in control. We had a rash of break-ins around the neighborhood a few months back. After that I upgraded this system with the latest technology. And I arranged to have new monitoring systems installed for several of my neighbors who were worried. Made us all feel more secure."

"It makes me feel a little uneasy."

"Don't be concerned. For instance, if you were out walking Jasmine on the property and something happened to you, I could find you very easily. I can't lose you. Not ever."

She heard his sudden intake of breath, followed by a long sigh. Rushing to change the subject, she said, "That reminds me. I need the code for the door, to turn off the alarm."

"Absolutely." He grinned up at her. "But before I do that. I want you to learn how to operate this system."

"Gus, I don't know. I'm not good at technical things."

"You'll learn. Pull up a chair. I have something special for you," he said.

She brought a chair over from along the wall and sat down beside him, still fascinated by all the computer screens. "Am I going to have to learn all this?"

"Not the business stuff, unless you want to. But I think

you need to know how the cameras work. Watch me," he said, and he began to explain how the cameras on the system worked.

"I'm not going to remember any of this," she said, feeling a little anxious.

"It will take time for you to learn all this. But for now, I want you to understand the basics."

He explained things too quickly for her to follow, but she didn't want to ask him to slow down. As she watched him, she decided that she would learn as much as she could about all this. Not today, certainly, but soon. As she sat near him she regretted that she had very little experience with tech stuff, always leaving it to Grace to figure out. She only used a couple of functions on her phone because those few met her needs. As she watched Gus, she realized that she had a lot more to learn.

When he finished, he reached over to the far corner of the desk. "I have something for you." He passed here a sleek new iPad. "If you're going to be shopping and looking at things, maybe making changes in the house, I thought you'd like to have a new iPad. It has a lot of applications for home design changes. I've loaded several really great apps on it to measure spaces, to search easily for sources of materials, whether online or in stores."

She laughed, holding up her hand. "Whoa! It all sounds complicated. I don't know if I can get the hang of so much technology."

"That's where I come in. I'm going to show you how to work all the apps, get you up to speed on all the important technology you'll need living here. Technology is the future. We all need to be knowledgeable. You included," he teased.

"Can I use it for reading books?"

"Of course. You download as many books as you want. It's set up on one of my credit cards. You can start anytime."

"Thank you. Really. And I love the books I found in my bedroom. I've never seen such a huge collection of Agatha Christie. I'm a huge fan. I'm looking forward to all the books shelved in the library."

He sobered. "I know this is going to sound strange to you, but I'd rather you didn't go in there."

"Why?"

"Because that's where I found Annabelle... When she died," he said in just above a whisper.

"Oh. I'm sorry. What a horrible thing to have happen. Of course, I won't go in there if you don't want me to. But Gus, if we're going to live here, you're going to have to accept what happened in that room."

"I know that. And I will, but for now, I need a little time. Do you understand?" he looked at her, his eyes dark and glistening.

Emily saw the pain in his eyes, and put her arm around him. She couldn't imagine coming home to find a lifeless Mark, the shock alone would have been devastating. "Is there anything I can do?"

"Just be here with me," he said, holding her close.

"Of course." They sat together, holding each other. All the while Emily was struggling to think of something that would ease the pain she'd seen in his eyes. "Why don't we do something? Go somewhere? Maybe have a picnic on the beach?"

He laughed. "The beaches here can be pretty chilly. The North Atlantic, you know."

"Is there a lake handy with a beach?" she asked.

"In fact, there is. Not far from here. Want to go now?"

"Right now? I've never just up and taken off to the beach on a whim," she said, trying to remember the last time she'd gone to a beach.

"You're serious?" he asked.

"Yes."

"Well, let's remedy that." He took her hand and they climbed the stairs.

"Yes. Let's. I'll put together a small picnic and we'll go."

It took time to find things in an unfamiliar kitchen, but she managed to put together a few crackers, cheese, grapes and Gus chose a bottle of wine to add to the basket. "This is a great idea. I never seem to find the time to go to the beach with so much going on in my life," he said.

"And it's no fun going alone," she added.

He looked at her for a few minutes. "Nothing's much fun when you're doing it alone."

The drive to the lake took them through long stretches of wooded areas, along narrow roads that ran ribbonlike, wrapping around hilly areas, until Gus turned down a narrow road. The rhythmic swipe and patter of branches against the side window of the car felt different somehow than the night she'd arrived. Had it really been only a few days ago?

She still hadn't talked to Gus about the poor reception on her phone, and instead had taken delight in sitting in the secret garden with Jasmine by her side as she talked to Grace. Why hadn't she mentioned it to him? Was she embarrassed about her lack of knowledge? Or maybe she worried that the answer was something very simple and it was she who, once again, didn't understand technology.

Suddenly, they burst out of the trees and into a wide-open expanse of sand with the water shining bright blue just feet away. "What a wonderful spot," she said, as she gazed up at the boughs of tall birch trees, at their white trunks, at their glossy leaves fluttering in the gentle breeze.

"There's a picnic table over there," Gus said, striding ahead, carrying the basket.

They unpacked the basket, settling in beside each other facing the water. As he poured wine into two plastic wine glasses, she noted the thick hair on his forearms, the way his hands pulled the cork from the bottle.

He passed her a glass. "To us."

"To us," she said, feeling the breeze on her face, hearing the gentle lap of water along the shoreline. *Could it be any more perfect than this?*

They gazed out at the water as they ate. Emily pointed out several different plants that she recognized from the books on native plants she'd found in the living room.

"How do you know all these things?" he asked.

"Books. The Internet."

He hugged her. "You take everything seriously, don't you?"

"I want to be part of your life here. It's such a beautiful place. And I want to go to the parks, especially Gros Morne National Park."

"We'll do that someday soon. I promise. Let's go down to the water."

They walked together, the sun suddenly peeking out of the clouds. "What a beautiful sight," she sighed, hugging his arm as they walked. He was much taller than she, making her feel protected by him. Mark had been a smaller man.

"Can you skip a rock?" she asked, feeling playful.

"What?"

"Let me show you." She spotted a small flat smooth stone near the water's edge. She picked it up, angled it in her fingers and threw it out across the water. It ran parallel to the surface before touching down on the water, dipping up, touching down again and again.

"Where did you learn to do that?" he asked, a look of surprise on his handsome features.

"I used to do it as a kid. Taught Grace to do it, but she's not really a beach kind of person," she said, happy to have impressed him. "Want me to teach you?"

"Sure."

She found another rock and showed him how to do it. His concentration was fierce, his attention unwavering as he pushed her to show him more. Within minutes he had it right, sending a rock skittering across the water as if he'd done it all his life.

"You are amazing," she said.

He looked out over the water for a few minutes, then back at her. "Thanks for showing me how to do that." He gave her an assessing glance, that made her feel...watched.

His eyes never left hers, his gaze never wavered. He'd never looked at her quite that way before. Nervously, she said, "Let's go back and enjoy our wine."

Once seated beside each other, he turned to her. "I feel I should explain a little about Annabelle. I know I told you about her in one of our conversations, but now that you're here, you need to know more of the story." He toyed with the stem of his glass. "She had a bad heart. She'd been on medication for years when I met her. I fell in love with her, and wanted to marry her and take care of her. I'd only moved to Newfoundland a few months before I met her. Wasn't sure I'd stay because Penny was still in Ontario with her daughter and I was worried I might be too lonely to stay.

"But Annabelle changed all that. We decided to marry. Penny was concerned that I was taking on a lot of responsibility, but when she saw how much in love we were, she understood." He sipped his wine. "I always knew the day would come, but I wanted to be near Annabelle and care for her. She had no family to care for her."

"She was very lucky to have found you. To have someone care the way you did." She touched his arm, his bare skin trembling beneath her touch.

"I was the lucky one," he said.

As she gazed into his eyes, she realized that she loved this man more now than ever.

"Being together like this has made such a difference," she said, as he turned to face her.

There was that look again, as if he could see right into her soul. She'd never experienced such a look in her life. It made her feel naked, open in ways she hadn't felt before...as if he knew something she didn't.

Stop doing this to yourself! This is Gus. The man you love.

"Emily, I want to make love to you."

"Here?" She gave an embarrassed laugh. She'd waited for days for him to want to make love, and now her reaction was coming across like that of a silly woman.

"No. In my room where you belong. I know we've had separate rooms since you got here, but I want to change that," he said, his hands coming up around her throat, his fingers treading the skin on her neck, gently, softly, driving her crazy with need.

"I...I want to make love to you too," she whispered, her body arching to his.

"Then, what are we waiting for?" he whispered close to her ear.

"I have no idea," she said.

Quickly, they gathered up the basket, hurried to the car and headed back to the house. Neither said anything until they drove into the garage. "Leave the basket here. I don't want to wait," he said, getting out of the vehicle, pressing his thumb to the keypad, waving her in ahead of him. They went into the kitchen, his arms around her, holding her close, kissing her, driving her crazy with need.

"I've waited for this, wanted to do this at the airport when you arrived. Just pull you into a closet or behind the carrousel," he whispered, nipping her shoulder through the thin fabric. "Waited so long..."

Suddenly, the front door crashed open. A tall woman with fiery red hair stood, tears streaming down her face.

"You've got to help me!" she yelled, coming across the floor and flinging her arms around Gus's neck.

Emily stepped back, surprised and shocked.

Gus held the woman at arm's length. "Emily, this is my daughter, Penny," he said with emphasis. "What are you doing here in the middle of a work day?" he demanded of the woman clinging to him.

Emily could see the grip he had on his daughter's arms, the tendons in his hands straining against his skin. Father and daughter stared at each other, neither making a move. The woman was rail thin, but heavily muscled, as if she worked out every day. Penny seemed oblivious to the fact that Emily was standing there, never once looking her way.

"Penny, it's nice to meet you," she said, not sure if it was or not. Gus had never mentioned Penny having emotional issues, but this woman was more than simply upset.

"I need to talk to you, *Dad. Alone.*" Penny's eyes never left Gus's face as she beat her hands on his chest.

"Go down to my office and I'll be right there," he said, as if to a child.

She stomped off down the stairs, leaving Gus and Emily staring at each other. "I apologize for my daughter. She's had a rough few weeks at work. Big deal going down, and someone in the office has been making trouble for her."

"I understand. Daughters can be a handful at times," she said to console him. But she didn't understand at all. Grace had never, ever behaved that way. The woman definitely had problems.

"I may be a little while. When Penny's upset..." He shrugged, giving her a what-can-I-do look.

Emily watched him follow his daughter down the stairs, a thought running through her mind. For someone Gus claimed to love and worry about, there was only two photos of his daughter in the house; one along the wall leading to the front door and one in his bedroom. She'd gone in his bedroom the other day to open the drapes and let the light in, only to find very little in the way of personal things on the armoire or the dresser, other than the photos of Tessa and Penny.

There was a lovely, framed photo of his granddaughter Tessa in the living room, one along the hall next to Penny's photo, and in his bedroom.

Emily had many photos of Grace, from the time she was a child right up to a few weeks before she left Boston. Why wouldn't there be photos of his only daughter all over the house? Or was she over-analyzing, from the time she was young, through high school and college? Maybe other parents didn't fill their house with photos of their only daughter like she did.

Still wondering about what she'd just witnessed, Emily went up to her room. She'd have a shower while she waited for Penny to leave. Having witnessed Penny's behavior, she really wasn't sure she wanted the woman around.

CHAPTER FOUR

"Get a grip on yourself," Gus demanded as he watched his wife slamming around his office, kicking the walls, spinning his desk chair as she circled the room. At least the space was sound proof, which meant that Emily couldn't hear this insanity. "What in hell are you doing here?"

"You. I'm here for you. And I saw that horny look in your eyes. You were headed upstairs to give her a good screwing, weren't you?" She spit the words at him. "We're in this together, or have you forgotten?"

"I haven't. We've been together since our time in British Columbia."

"Where I got you a new ID at that crazy hospital where I worked. The first time we killed, that stupid woman you befriended in Kamloops. Remember? You and I are good together. You said so. We share the same things, me and you." She jabbed the air with her fist as she marched back and forth across the room.

"Yes, and we're going to share more." He tried for a calm tone. "Emily is going to be our biggest event yet. She's perfect."

"Is that why she took so long? All the pandering to her on Zoom. The lies you spun. You enjoyed it way too much. And I've been as patient as I can. But we need to do this." She stopped in front of him, her hands on his chest. "I've given my life to you, to us, to this need thing we share. You told me we'd always have this just for us. I need to do this. I'm tired of waiting."

"I know. But it's going to be worth it. Trust me."

"I'm fucking tired of you having all the fun. Why do you have to sleep with her? Why can't you pretend to be impotent?" Penny pushed her hands up over his chest, dug her nails into his neck, shoved her body against his, and kissed him, biting down hard on his lip.

"That hurt!" he said, fighting to control his anger. He wanted to hit her, but if he did he'd leave a red welt on his wife's face. And if Emily saw that...he didn't have a lie that would cover brutalizing his 'daughter'.

"You rotten bastard! I'm sitting over in that miserable condo waiting for you to finish the plan and you're over here enjoying yourself."

"Cut it out!" He crushed her hands in his. "Do you hear me? This is my business. Not yours." He growled, squeezing harder.

Tears shone in her eyes, her face contorted. "That's a lie! I've been part of this since Vancouver. You were just a poor orderly in the mental hospital, and I got you a clean identity when that old man died. I took the risk by not turning in the paperwork on him until we were ready to leave the province. My brains got you started in all this. Not yours. I was the one who figured out that we needed to move to Alberta so we didn't leave a trail. I was the one who figured out that we could kill anyone we pleased, if we did it right."

"You were very helpful, and you still are. But we can't take any chances with this one." He softened his tone. "We've done it right for years. You and me. And we've enjoyed every minute. Together, we're unstoppable."

"Then, listen to me. Stop jerking around and let's get this one finished." She yanked her hands from his, her eyes blazing malice.

"Calm down."

"Make me." She slapped him across the mouth.

He hit her in the ribs, knocked her to the floor, watched her writhe around. "I want you to listen to me," he said, placing one foot on her ankle.

He wiped his lip, feeling the raw skin and tasting the saltiness of blood. They'd been through this before. Her fury, the demands, the crying and finally the pleading for him to have sex with her. "I've got a different plan for this one."

"No. We're going to follow through, get it over." She gasped out the words as she glared at him from the floor. She made no move to get up.

"As we decided many times before, Penny, the key to our success is that we never commit the same kill twice in the same way. We've used different chemicals, different weapons, different methods, all to keep ahead of the law. We're good together. That won't change. But you have to be patient, just a little longer."

"Meaning?' she asked, getting slowly to her feet, going to lean against the wall near the computers.

"We need to watch and wait. You were right; Millie Hansen was a good test case for our new way to capture *clients*." He had to praise her, get her to settle down. "Your plan to dispose of her body in the bird sanctuary was brilliant. No one will think to look there, so isolated out in the middle of nowhere. While the wonderful Royal Newfoundland Constabulary are going batshit looking for her, thinking she's gone up north for a holiday, they won't have the resources to check into anything we've got going on now."

"Yeah," Penny rubbed her ribs, her eyes cold. "But this whole idea of getting women off a dating site is way too complicated. We need to keep the plan simple. Find them. Befriend them. Get them to trust us. Then kill them."

But he wasn't being entirely honest. Recently he had acted on his own, taking all the pleasure for himself without her. She'd go berserk if she knew. A trickle of fear ran through him...but he tamped it down.

Penny must never find out about the two women in the pet cemetery. For the first time since they'd started their life together, he'd found himself frantic to kill. He wasn't proud of his loss of control, but he vowed it wouldn't happen again. He and Penny had a good working relationship, one he didn't intend to ruin.

"I think we need to adjust our strategy just a little. We have to look at the big picture. If we find them on a dating site, we don't have to be seen with them until we're ready to close in on them. We pick women who are lonely, looking for love and attention. I've learned a lot about how to manipulate women on a dating site. They're so eager to please, practically pleading to meet up. Millie and now Emily have been easy so far. Millie was the test case for the online method. She wanted to meet up so badly she came to St. John's and moved into an apartment, met me wherever I wanted to meet, then told her family back in Boston that she was going on a trip for a few weeks," he said, patiently, trying to keep Penny calm. "She was almost too easy. But Emily is a little different. I got this house from Annabelle when we did her, and I plan to set up my retirement plan off Emily."

"You mean our retirement plan," Penny said, her voice rising.

"Yes, our retirement plan," he said, forcing his voice to remain flat, controlled.

"Fine. But you've already spent hours making nice to her

on the phone, on email and using all your other devices. How much longer?" She pushed off from the wall, running her hands through the mass of red curls.

He'd always liked the way she looked when she was upset. Her aggression, her behavior that bordered on unstable was a turn on. He loved bringing her back under control. "Penny, Emily has serious money. We want it. Tessa will need it when it's time for her to go away to school. Think about our daughter and her future. Think about the house we've talked about owning in the Bahamas. Think about the trips we can take, once the money is secure."

"Oh, for God's sake! Don't use that line on me. We've got lots of money!" She started pacing the room again. "This is supposed to be a partnership. It doesn't feel like one to me." She pouted, her tear-stained cheeks flushed, her eyes searching his.

He knew what she wanted, but he had to grab the opportunity while the vulnerability shone in her eyes. "Not this kind of money. Listen to me. I need time. Let Emily think we're going to be married. I'll propose to her if I have to. I need to have the legal documents drawn up to have her leave me everything."

"You've done it before, many times... For years," Penny said quietly. "Why keep her alive any longer? What's different with this one?"

"You're not listening to me. Until recently we simply chose women, based on our needs and their availability. Killing's been to satisfy us. For our pleasure. But things have changed. From now on, money is also a consideration. If we want, we'll have money to expand, maybe start operating out of the Bahamas, change the pattern and the location."

Seeing the flash of interest in her eyes, he said, "In Annabelle's case it was easy. I married her. And she was so grateful she left me everything. I don't want to lose my touch.

Getting Millie's money was easy too, no interfering children and a test run for the online...shall we say...procurement of our victims."

"You're liking this a whole lot more than you used to. Something changed?" Penny asked.

He stared hard at her, reaching for the old control he'd exerted on her all these years.

"Online is the future in our business. We just have to go slowly, get it right. Not make a mistake. This one has a daughter who's a lawyer. I have to be careful not to trigger a lot of questions. I gave Emily an iPad that allows me to track what she's doing. Her phone doesn't work near the house, which means her daughter can't tell when she's physically in here. Something I may have to make use of...keeping my options open. She hasn't complained to me about it yet."

"Why not? What's wrong with the bitch?"

"Nothing's wrong. She's just anxious, not wanting to upset me. She'll do anything to please me. I want to keep her that way. When she does bring it up, I'll give her a new phone so I can track her calls, texts. Much more efficient."

"What about me? I hate the real estate business. I hate pretending to be your daughter, seeing you only when it works for you. I've spent the last two days trying to pretend you weren't here with her, and when I come to see you, you're headed upstairs with her."

Penny's voice rose, her eyes widened in disgust. "Two can play at this game. I'm going to find the next victim, my way. And that means I'll be hitting the bars, bringing men home, having sex—"

He grabbed her hair, pulled hard, bringing her face to his. "Don't even think about bringing any trash anywhere near Tessa. She must never be exposed to any of your bad behavior. I have to put up with your wantonness, but she doesn't. If you do anything to involve her in this, you'll be sorry." He glared at her, his fingers pinching the skin on her arms, raising ugly welts.

Penny swallowed. Tears welled up in her eyes. Her mouth worked. She said nothing.

He patted her arm, releasing his grip on her hair. "We've been in this for years, you and me. There have been times when I've had to have sex with the women to control them, to get them to do what I wanted."

"More times than not!" She pointed her finger at him. Her eyes wild, her lips trembling, she rounded on him.

He knew what came next. What had to come next. His wife needed rough sex, sex that left her hurting. He'd done it every time she got upset over a victim. The woman's jealousy was such a driving force, and one he had to manage, for Tessa's sake. Nothing could happen to his daughter while she lived away from him with his wife.

He'd do anything, including sexually assaulting his wife, to keep her from going off the deep end. But the day was coming when she would also have to be dealt with once and for all.

But he didn't want to upset Tessa any more than necessary. Tessa was the only thing in the world that meant anything to him. It wasn't that he'd experienced the love everyone gushed about. It was that she was his, his seed, what would be left when he was gone. He would do whatever it took to keep his child safe. He'd set up monitoring systems all over the condo Penny and Tessa lived in and was ready to intervene at a moment's notice, should Penny's violent behavior be directed at Tessa.

He hoped it didn't come to that. He would postpone any action against his wife as long as he could because his daughter seemed to genuinely love her mother. And if that's what Tessa needed for now, he'd be sure she had it.

But if Penny's behavior became more erratic, he wouldn't hesitate to act.

"Come here, lover." He reached for her hand.

She came willingly, her mouth open, her hands tearing at his clothes. He would make certain that she left here tattered and sated, through the back entrance of the basement. Then, he'd go up and blanket Emily with phony apologies.

All in a day's work.

Twenty minutes later, he ushered a spent woman through the door, careful to keep a tissue on the bleeding scratch on his chest where Penny clung to him as he beat her nearly senseless, after forcing her to have sex in the usual aberrant ways. His wife loved it all. But this incessant need to give her what she considered proof of his love was growing tiresome.

He had to get back upstairs with a solid excuse for being delayed so long, pleading the emotional upset he'd had dealing with his daughter. And thanks to his wife Penny he'd have to make excuses about the sex he planned to have with Emily. He couldn't have straight sex with the woman, knowing he'd have to explain the blood oozing from his chest. He grabbed a bandage from the medicine cupboard in the bathroom off his office, took a deep cleansing breath and went upstairs.

Emily was sitting on a stool at the island in the kitchen pretending to read the paper. But she wasn't. He could tell. "Sorry for all that. Penny just received bad news. The deal she was counting on fell through. I may have to help her out financially. She's embarrassed about her behavior and let herself out through the basement door."

Emily stared at him. "We need to talk," she said.

"What is it, darling?" he said, hurrying to her side.

. . .

After a long shower, Emily had spent the last hour and a half wondering what was going on in Gus's office. She'd tiptoed to the top of the stairs, but could hear nothing. She was suspicious, to say the least. If Penny was that upset, how come she couldn't hear any sound? No yelling. No crying. Nothing.

She put the newspaper down. "Gus, I accepted that because of Penny and her situation, I had to move here while we worked out our living arrangements. Against my daughter's advice I came here. I've waited to meet your daughter and Tessa, and it hasn't happened. Until today when she arrives here unannounced and makes a scene."

"Sorry about that," he said, ducking his head.

"You're hurt," she said. "The side of your mouth is bleeding."

"I must have scratched too hard. Happens sometimes... aging skin, I guess." He turned away, reached into a side cupboard for a tissue, dabbing the spot.

"Look, I realize that this is new to Penny. She probably cared a great deal for Annabelle, but—"

"She was upset," he said, coming to sit beside her, his hand covering hers.

What happened to his mouth? Did his daughter hit him? No. It couldn't be. Gus wasn't the sort of man who would take that behavior from anyone, certainly not from his daughter. *Would he?* "Too upset to be civil? She didn't even acknowledge my existence."

He squeezed her fingers gently. "Penny can be very difficult. And I apologize. I should have called her on it, made her behave better. She certainly knows better. Her mother and I were very strict with her... Maybe too strict."

Emily pulled her hand from under his. The way he covered for his daughter was offensive, given that Emily had come all this way to be with him. He definitely had a red spot on his lip. It would seem that he didn't have any control over this woman. "You've never told me exactly what Penny's problem is."

"She hates her job."

"Then, get her to quit."

"It isn't that simple." There was a strange look in his eyes, one she hadn't seen before.

"Is it a money issue? You have lots of money."

"It's not a money issue at all. She's just a little high strung."

"And rude."

"Yes. Rude." He dabbed the red spot on his face, his eyes focused on the wall across the room.

She'd never seen him like this before, withdrawn and sort of angry, maybe. It was difficult to read his expression. "Gus, I hate to say this, but your daughter needs professional help."

"Look, I'm really sorry about all this. I will speak to Penny about her behavior. Can we forget it for now? Why don't we go into the city, to an art gallery, maybe have dinner? Or would you like to take a drive to Citadel Hill? It's a beautifully restored historic site. What do you say?"

Emily sighed. "It's clear to me that you have issues you have to resolve with your daughter. I don't want to be caught in the middle, that's all."

"You won't be. I promise you I will work things out with Penny. You matter a great deal to me. I love you," he murmured close to her ear.

"I love you, too, Gus. We both have to be patient with our daughters until they understand that we aren't giving up on each other. That we're truly together. You will work this out with her, won't you?"

He nodded.

CHAPTER FIVE

Twice the following week Penny called and asked to speak to her father. Not one word of apology to Emily. The woman's behavior was beyond annoying, and the next time Penny entered the house, she would speak to her. No matter what excuse Gus gave for his daughter, Emily was through pretending there wasn't a problem.

Two days ago, when he'd gotten back from the women's shelter where he did volunteer work, she decided to bring up the subject of his daughter. She'd just gotten off the phone with Penny, furious with her behavior, and told him so. Gus had shown genuine anger over his daughter, and had disappeared to his office for an hour. When he returned, he said nothing about what he did, or even if he'd talked to Penny.

She was disappointed that he hadn't been more open about what he'd done about her, whether he had a reasonable conversation with her about her behavior. She'd waited several days and still he'd said nothing.

But aside from the issues around Penny's behavior, life with Gus was wonderful in so many ways. He was kind, caring, and his lovemaking the other night was wonderful.

She'd never felt more completely loved in her entire life. She found that hard to admit even to herself. All the years she'd been married to Mark, their lovemaking had been pleasant, even fun sometimes, but never the mind-bending experience that lovemaking was with Gus.

She sighed. Yet there remained a few niggling problems. The cell phone issue. She still had to leave the house and walk out toward the road to get good reception, which was where she was headed at the moment. Snapping the leash on Jasmine, she walked through the door into the bright sunshine.

And that reminded her of the other issue. She couldn't lock the door because she had no code to get back in. Oh, well, she couldn't expect things to be perfect overnight. She'd only been there a couple of weeks. And aside from Penny everything had been great between them. She would give Gus time to work out his issues with his daughter. If she was having the same sort of problem with Grace, she'd expect him to understand and be supportive.

She started down the drive with Jasmine and this time she didn't go into the secret garden, but stayed on the driveway while she dialed Grace's number. Grace answered on the first ring.

"How's it going, Mom?"

"Great. Nothing new since yesterday, except the usual. Penny's causing a little problem."

"Still?"

"Yes, she threw a hissy fit the other day. Very embarrassing for Gus."

"What about you? How did you feel?"

"Annoyed. I think Penny is very spoiled."

"And probably pissed that her father has a new woman in his life."

"But she's known about me all along."

"Mom, I've known about Gus, and had issues with what is going on. And Gus didn't move into your house and set up housekeeping."

"Whose side are you on?" she joked.

"Just saying. Anyway, it'll work out. Or it won't. How are things otherwise?"

"Well, my cell phone reception at the house isn't very good."

"Meaning?"

"I can't call from the house. I tried to call you the other day. Yesterday I tried to call Millie Hansen, the friend I told you was now living in Newfoundland, and the call didn't go through. I went to the garden to call her daughter, and she said her mom had taken a trip up to Labrador with the man she met. Can't remember his name. But it doesn't matter right now. I'm sure Millie will call when she gets back to St. John's. Now that she knows I'm here, she and I will get together."

"Mom, it does matter. All of it matters. What's going on there? You should be able to call from the house. That's dangerous if you're alone in the house and can't make a call. You told me that his house is isolated. Anything could happen and you wouldn't be able to call anyone."

"I know. But I'm not sure what I should do."

"What does Gus say?"

"I haven't told him, yet."

"Mom! You used to do this all the time with Dad. Have a problem and not tell him. Not that I'm a big fan of this relationship, as you know, but you do owe it to Gus to tell him what is going on with your phone. He's a techie person. There's no reason he would want your phone not to work."

"Did you get my email I sent you from my new iPad?"

"When did you send it?"

"Two days ago."

"That one? Yes. Why are you asking?"

"Because it took so long for it to go out, or seemed to."

There was a pause, then Grace came back on the line. "Mom, I've pulled over so we can talk about this. Gus ran a very successful tech security firm. Why would you have trouble using any piece of technology inside his home?"

"I don't know."

"Well, I assume you can manage the security system. I remember him telling you all about it. Has he put you on the system, given you a code?"

"Not yet. He uses a code, or his thumb print."

"You'd better find out what the code is as soon as you can. You need to be able to get in and out of the house and to lock it when you leave."

"You're right. I will."

"How's it going otherwise?"

"Great. We are very compatible, like so many of the same things. He's a really good driver, even in fog. He likes to play cribbage, and he's good at it. I taught him to skip a stone on the water."

"Just like you taught me, Mom. I'm happy for you. I mean that. Gus isn't my type. But who is these days? Just want the best for you. That's all. I've got to go now. Talk tomorrow?"

"Yes. Love you."

"Love you, too."

When Grace hung up, Emily was suddenly overwhelmed with loneliness. She wanted to see Grace, to go to lunch in Boston with her, hear her talk about her work. She missed her home back in Boston too, her kitchen with its clean lines and carefully planned space. Very different from Gus's huge kitchen with every conceivable appliance known to mankind.

But isn't it normal to be a little lonely for home?

Maybe she'd talk to Gus about it when he got back. He'd

left early to do banking for the shelter and pick up their mail. He seemed to have many routine duties for the organization, and she supposed that with any organization like the shelter, running short of volunteers, everyone had to pitch in. And in truth she was just really happy to know he had something worthwhile that he was passionate about.

Which reminded her. They hadn't purchased the bench for the garden. Once she walked Jasmine she'd drive to the landscaping place and see what she could find. Theresa would be along any minute... She'd tell her where she was going.

But first, she'd walk along the road with Jasmine. She'd discovered a walking path a little farther along where she could go deep into the woods to a small brook where Jasmine liked to have a drink.

When she got back to the house, Theresa was cleaning the kitchen. "What a beautiful day for a walk," she said, as Theresa turned to greet her.

"It's lovely here, isn't it?"

"It is." Emily shrugged out of her jacket and unclipped Jasmine's leash. "I'm going to town for an hour or so. Is there anything I can pick up for you? Any cleaning things?"

"No. But I'll be gone when you get back. I have a dentist appointment. I'll come back and finish up this afternoon. I already told Mr. Parsons."

"That's a bit of a problem. I don't have the code for getting back in the house. In fact, I don't know how to set the alarm," she said, feeling a little foolish.

"Not a problem. I'll show you, and give you my code so you can lock up when you leave," Theresa said, going to the keypad and showing her the settings, turning on the alarm, before using the code to deactivate the alarm. "I... I don't know how Mr. Parsons will feel about me telling you this. He said my code was just for me, no one else. I think he worries too much about security."

"I agree with you. I'd planned to ask him about it this morning. I'll be sure to ask him this evening. See you later this afternoon."

A couple of hours later, Emily hummed to herself as she drove back down the road leading to Gus's house. She'd had a lovely hour with one of the employees at the landscaping company, and she found a bench she really loved. With a dog that looked like a spaniel engraved on the backrest of the bench it would be perfect for the pet cemetery. She'd get Gus to go with her to see it later that afternoon. Then, she'd treat him to dinner somewhere in St. John's.

She glanced in the rearview mirror to see a large SUV very much like Gus's behind her. She smiled to herself as she rolled down the window and waved to him. The vehicle slowed behind her, flashing its headlights. She waved and pulled over. She watched Gus get out of his vehicle, his tall angular body draped to perfection in a camel hair coat. His gold-and-brown flecked cashmere scarf made him look incredibly handsome.

"Hi, what a nice surprise," she said, as he came up to her window.

"I was worried about you, dear. I called the house, and you weren't there. I called your cell phone and you didn't answer," he said, leaning into the window, turning his head as he looked past her for just a minute.

What is he looking at? She touched her cheek self-consciously. "I'm sorry. I decided to go into town to look for a bench. I found one, and wondered if you'd be interested to see it later this afternoon."

"Sure... I need to go to the house first, then we can go

together." He stepped back, a frown on his face as he seemed to stare at her. Why don't you follow me to the house?"

He got back in his vehicle and roared down the road ahead of her.

What was going on with that look he gave her? Something didn't feel right. Had something happened at the shelter?

She pulled into the garage next to him and got out of the vehicle. "I want to buy you dinner this evening. We need an outing."

"That would be nice," he said, distractedly pressing his thumb into the key pad. He opened the door and strode into the kitchen, putting a brown paper bag on the counter.

She came in behind him. "I think it would be fun to meet someone in town for a drink or something. We need to get out and meet people."

"Certainly," he said, his eyes suddenly on her. "Emily, are you okay?"

"Yes. I'm fine. I do wonder though if I might have a problem with my cell phone."

"What's that?"

"I can't get decent reception here at the house. If I walk down the driveway nearly to the road, or into the secret garden I can use my phone just fine."

"Oh! I have a lot of security features here at the house that sometimes interfere with my phone as well. I need to do something about that," he said, taking her hand, his smile wrapping around her. "I have a surprise for you."

"A surprise?"

"Yes. I bought a new iPhone for you the week before you arrived. I wanted to give it to you, but thought the earrings were more appropriate. But since you brought up the issue of cell reception, I think it is time I gave it to you."

"You don't have to do that. As long as I can make a few calls home from here, that's all I need."

"No. I want you to have all the best technology. After all, you're involved with a man involved in the tech business. It makes sense that you have all the bells and whistles."

He led her down to his office where he presented her with a new phone. "I want you to have that with you no matter where you go. Promise me you'll keep the phone with you. It'll be like I'm with you."

"I promise," she said, acutely aware of him, of his physical presence; sometimes a little overwhelming.

He stroked her cheek, his scent surrounding her, his eyes intent. "I didn't mean to be so cool with you out on the street, but when I couldn't reach you I was afraid something had happened to you." He gave her a wan smile. "I don't know what I'd do if anything happened to you. That's why I want you to keep the phone on you at all times," he said, his fingers moving over her throat as he looked into her eyes.

You walk out of the house without your phone, and I don't know where you've gone. Penny got what she wanted this morning. Now, I'm going to have what I want.

"Why don't we go upstairs for a while," he whispered close to her ear, sending tingles of need down her spine.

"What about Theresa? Isn't she supposed to be back here this afternoon after her dental appointment?"

"You're right. I forgot all about it," he said. "But we have this evening."

"After dinner out?"

"Absolutely. In the meantime, give me your phone and I'll transfer all the data for you. Then you'll be all set."

"Can we talk for a few minutes?" Emily asked.

"Sure," he said, taking the new phone out of the box and stripping all the wrapping from it.

"I'm really worried about Penny. I mean she seems to have issues way beyond simply being upset about her work."

He looked at her for a few minutes, until Emily began to

feel uneasy. "I don't mean to make any trouble between you and your daughter, but if I'm going to be part of your life, I'll also be part of hers. I want to have a good relationship with your daughter and your granddaughter."

"Oh, honey, I haven't been very upfront with you about Penny." He put the phone down and took her hands in his. "I am all Penny has. She wanted to stay with her mother in Ontario after her mother and I divorced. But she has always struggled with holding down a job. When Tessa was born, things changed for her. She wanted to be here with me. I knew I could support her and Tessa financially until she got settled and I did. Maybe the wrong thing to do, but I felt it was right at the time. After all, I had sold my business in Ontario and bought another business here. It has done really well, and when I saw an opportunity to sell it and remain a consultant for the business, I grabbed it. But whatever businesses I had I worked hard at, which meant that I didn't have much time for Penny...never did when she was growing up especially." He gave her an ingratiating grin. "Sorry for going on like this."

She squeezed his arm gently. "I remember how that was with Mark. He would work such long hours," she offered.

"Being an only child, and trying to raise a child on her own, Penny often felt overwhelmed. Things went from bad to worse, and finally I moved her here, close to me. I'm trying not to involve myself too much in her life. After all she's an adult with a child. You know how it is," he said, taking her hand in his.

"I do. Grace has certainly caused me concern at times, and she doesn't have a child. What about Tessa's father? Is he in the picture?"

"No. Unfortunately, he was a married man. Penny never really talked about him, and given how easily she gets upset, I didn't push it."

"Is there anything I can do? Could we plan dinner together some night? Maybe if we spent time together, and got to know each other a little better... Do you think?"

He gave her a sad smile. "No. Leave me to work on it. I promise if I need your help, I'll get you involved."

Why did Gus seem to feel he couldn't take any action where Penny was concerned? She certainly wouldn't allow Grace to behave the way Penny did. Gus didn't seem like the kind of man who put up with rude and difficult behavior from anyone.

They went out to dinner that evening after buying the bench. Gus couldn't have been more attentive. Emily was relieved to see that they were enjoying each other's company the way they'd done all those evenings on FaceTime and Zoom. He showed her some of the features on the new phone. He was such a wonderful teacher, kind and patient. She loved that about him.

"Honey, are you having a good evening?" he asked, as he passed her phone back to her.

"Yes. Of course. We always have such a good time when we're together."

"I was just wondering. You seemed a little...distracted earlier."

"No. I just want everything to be good between us. And I didn't mean to pry about Penny. You know her better than anyone. And I'm sure the time will come when she and I can be friends. I simply need to be patient."

"And relax. We have lots to look forward to. I want us to go to church this Sunday so my friends can meet you. And there are a couple of social events coming up you might enjoy." He played with her fingers, an eager smile on his face. "I want to show you off to people."

She smiled back at him, feeling the tension slide away. "That would be wonderful. I can't hide out in your house forever." She touched his face, lovingly.

If you only knew.... My PI confirmed what you're worth, much more than I expected. I should have known you wouldn't lie to me. You haven't yet, but it's nice to be sure. Only problem, my dear naïve Emily, Penny wants to move on to our next victim, some woman she found through the Chamber of Commerce, newly arrived in St. John's. No family. Just perfect. And Penny has to have what she wants.

As for you, first I get your daughter out of your life, then I propose. Then it's bye, bye Emily.

CHAPTER SIX

Though the evening had been lovely, as Emily snapped the leash on Jasmine's collar the next morning, she couldn't shake her concern around Gus's evasiveness over Penny.

How could she have such a hold on him? And why in heaven's name did he refuse to have his family to dinner?

She'd tried to speak with him about it again that morning, but he simply put her off, saying he had to get to the offices of Primo Technologies because Peter wanted his input on a client. That was the other thing that was bothersome. Gus worked all the time, either at the women's shelter or his business.

She grabbed her new phone and started down the driveway with Jasmine to where they had placed the bench yesterday. It was a lovely spot in the corner of the garden. The landscapers had worked into the evening and cleared a few wild shrubs that allowed her to sit looking at both gardens. Emily had assumed they'd do the work at a later date, but Gus had paid them extra to do it while they were out to dinner. He could be so kind, wonderful and attentive. Yet...

Settling in, the sun warming her, she called Grace.

When Grace picked up the phone her tone was upbeat. "Hi Mom, how's it going?"

"It's going...good. We had dinner out last night, and it was lovely. I'm sitting on a new bench in the garden, and the sun is finally shining."

"You knew you were living in fog-land when you went there," Grace said, a soft chuckle in her voice.

"I know. Don't remind me. But on a brighter note Gus got me a new cell phone. It's really nice."

"Are you talking to me from the house?"

"No. I'm in the garden with Jasmine. It's... It's lovely here." She stared up into the canopy of trees, the light sparkling in rhythm with the fluttering leaves.

"So you still can't call from inside the house?"

"I haven't tried. I guess I've gotten in the habit of coming down to this garden to call you," she sighed, wishing her daughter wouldn't pressure her.

"You sound a little down. Are you okay?" Grace asked.

"I'm good. Really. What's new with you?"

"I'm up to my eyeballs in court cases. Thankfully I have really good help. Don't want to think what it would be like if I didn't. Oh. By the way, I had a call from Ed Mahone. He and his wife are interested in your house, when and if you're planning to sell."

Emily's heart jumped in her throat. "I...I don't know. I hadn't really thought about it. What did you tell them?"

"Nothing, Mom. I didn't want to tell them that you were away trying to figure out if you wanted to move to Newfoundland for good. But I also know that you talked about buying a condo here and selling your house. When Ed asked if you'd be interested, I said I'd talk to you. He seemed satisfied with that. I don't think you have to make any plans at the moment."

She and Mark had bought the house twenty-years ago. It had been the only place she really felt at home in her whole life, so many wonderful memories. Waves of loneliness washed over her. She swallowed, remembering how easily she'd made the decision to come there without thinking that if she stayed here, her life in Boston would be finished. Except for visiting Grace and meeting friends while she stayed in Grace's condo.

Now, here she was trying to fit into Gus's life, and feeling a little lost.

But wasn't she with Gus to see if she wanted to live with him in St. John's? Whether she and Gus wanted to stay in Newfoundland? Oh...dear... Had she really thought things through?

"I agree with you, Gracie. There's no rush on a decision. I can sell my house anytime I want to."

"Mom, are you sure everything's okay?"

"Why would you ask?"

"Well, when you left here, wild horses couldn't stop you. And suddenly after a few days you're sounding a little unsure."

"Not so much unsure as wondering about something."

"Go on."

"Well, Gus has all kinds of issues with his daughter, and he won't talk about them. And believe me, she is one difficult person. I really don't like her very much. But if we were to move home to Boston together, he would be free of her."

"I'm not following you. Now you think he'd be willing to move here?"

"I don't know...maybe...Just thinking out loud," she said.

"Remember that the reason you had to go there was that Gus couldn't leave his daughter."

"Yes. And I understood completely, at the time."

"So, you're thinking you and Gus would be happier moving here. But what if Penny simply follows her father?"

"That's possible. Gus told me that she followed him from Ontario after he bought the business here."

"So, she's willing to move wherever her father goes. I'm not a psychologist, but why would a daughter follow her father? Most adult children want a life free of parental influence." There was a long pause. "Mom, I think you and Gus have to work out how you're going to deal with Penny. It's tricky because she's family. But if Gus is willing to share with you what's going on, and given your nursing skills, I'm sure you can figure something out. Whoops! That's my other line. I've got to take this call. Talk to you tomorrow."

"Yeah, tomorrow…"

After Grace hung up, Emily sat there staring up at the branches moving gently above her head, feeling a need to simply be quiet and at peace. Yet, despite the peacefulness of the space, she couldn't seem to keep her thoughts away from Gus and Penny. What if Gus couldn't change how he behaved with Penny? What if Penny came between them to the point where they fought all the time? She couldn't be happy knowing that Penny could behave disrespectfully toward her and get away with it. That Gus would not take a stand where Penny was concerned.

Would Gus always defend his daughter, regardless of how she behaved?

She stared at her hands resting in her lap, the first sign of a headache looming. The past weeks had been stressful in many ways, but she had to believe it would all be worth it in the end. They loved each other. Surely, they'd be able to talk this out between them.

Jasmine's sudden bark brought her back to the present.

"Okay, girl, we're heading back to the house," she said,

suddenly remembering that she hadn't locked the door. She had to start doing that, even if she was still using the house-keeper's code.

Once back in the house, she put the kettle on and made a cup of tea from Gus's huge selection of tea packets. She'd never seen so many in one place. But it was like Gus to do everything in a big way. With her tea mug in hand, she curled up on the living room sofa, enjoying the view and reading the paper. The peace and the quiet of the room soothed her as she read.

There were a couple of advertisements for shops in downtown St. John's that she wanted to check out. The news was all local with just a half a page of international news. As she turned to put her cup on the coffee table a glint from something on the top of the book shelf caught her eye.

Going to the shelf, she reached up and took it down. It was a small black plastic box with what looked like a camera lens on it. There didn't seem to be a light on it, or any indication that it was working. She turned it over. Primo Tech was stamped on the back.

Why would Gus have something like that here in his living room? Maybe it wasn't a camera. She turned it over in her hands. There were no other marks on it. And the eye or lens had been pointed toward her when she picked it up. *What if it is a camera? Who keeps a camera in their living room? Is he spying on me?*

Surely not! She felt tense again. She'd ask Gus about it when he got home. Yet, how could she do that without sounding suspicious? But wouldn't anyone be suspicious about a security or snooping camera in the living room?

Stop doing this to yourself!

Wanting to put all those thoughts aside she went to the kitchen to start dinner, enthralled as usual with the very upscale features of the kitchen. In what she had decided to call the gadget cupboard, she found an air fryer. She'd never used one, but when she got to the instructions for baking chicken they seemed simple. Once she'd placed the chicken in the air fryer she settled on one of the stools.

Yet, she couldn't stop her eyes from searching the top of the cupboards, and along the counters. Was she really looking for another camera? No! Surely not.

But what was that thing? Were there more? She got up and went to the laundry area, looking for anything that resembled the thing in the living room.

She heard the back door open. Taking a deep breath, she gathered her thoughts. "Hi, how was your day?" she asked.

Gus walked into the kitchen, his hand behind his back. "It was good, but a little hectic. I wanted to make up for being away all day. I hadn't intended to be, but Peter and I had a lot to discuss, mostly about his plans for expansion of the business. I was busy. I didn't look at my watch." He passed her a large bouquet of red roses. "Just want you to know I love coming home to you."

"Oh. Gus. They're beautiful." She held them up to her face, the scent surrounding her. "Thank you."

He took her in his arms, and held her close – his strength, the solidness of him, a balm to her earlier worries. They were meant to be together. And they would be happy. She'd make sure of it. "I've organized dinner, chicken in the air fryer, carrots, potatoes and chocolate brownies. All diet, by the way."

He laughed. "How did you take the calories out of the brownies?"

"It's an imaginary low-cal brownie."

"Sounds great. I don't think I've ever used that air fryer. It was a gift from Penny a couple of years ago."

"Well, being a low-tech person, I had to read the entire

manual to figure out what was involved in roasting a chicken."

"You know that's one of my goals. I saw your hesitancy around your new phone. And your uncertainty around the iPad I gave you. I want you to be completely comfortable using technology, especially the technology you'll use every day."

"Speaking of that, I found something." She took his hand and led him into the living room. "What is that?" She pointed to the top of the bookshelf.

He stood perfectly still, his mouth working. "That's a camera."

"What's it doing there?" she asked, her shoulders tightening.

He sighed. "I should have removed it. I guess I forgot it was there. When Annabelle was ill, I put a camera in any room she'd be in while I was away from the house. I wanted to be able to see her. To talk directly to her. And her to me."

"But why not use one of those alarm bracelets linked to the phone system? If she fell, you'd know immediately."

He sighed again. "I don't know. Things were pretty difficult near the end and sometimes I wasn't thinking straight. I didn't tell you this, but in the last months my wife had a tracheotomy that scared me. I wanted to be able to see her when I wasn't here. If I checked the camera and she was reading, I was pleased. We tried to use FaceTime, but she couldn't hold the phone and talk. If she looked sad, I'd call her, try to cheer her up," he said, looking downcast.

It was Emily's turn to sigh. Feeling guilty about her suspicions, she turned toward him. "I'm sorry for everything you and your wife went through. To think she had a tracheotomy. It must have been frightening for you."

"It was. Never having been around medical things I was afraid it could get blocked somehow." He moved closer, looking down into her eyes, his breath soft on her cheek. "I hope you're not too upset. I wasn't spying on you. I wouldn't do that."

She saw the sadness in his eyes, and wanted to soothe his pain. "You were worried for her. You wanted to know she was safe when you weren't here," she said, his gaze so intense she had to look away.

"Let's not talk about this anymore, Emily. You've got dinner all organized, but we do have a little time," he said, his smile warm.

"What would you like to do?" she asked, happy to see him smile again.

He put his arms around her, drawing her close to him, making her feel safe. "I'd like to take you upstairs, make love to you," he murmured into her throat as his tongue moved over her heated skin.

Her body moved into his, her fingers knitted their way into his hair. "I'd like that too," she said, her body pressing against his.

"Then, what are we waiting for?" he asked, taking her hand and leading her upstairs to the bedroom. She followed him, her hand tightly gripped in his.

Why had she been so suspicious of him? Why didn't she simply relax and enjoy this time together? There were things in his life that would have to change, like the camera thing. And there were things in her life that would have to change; like she needed to start thinking as a couple, and not look for things to worry about.

The next morning, they were up and dressed and ready in plenty of time for church. She had been looking forward to this, to meeting some of his friends, getting to know about his life in the community. She knew he was a successful businessman, and she wanted to learn about those people, outside of his work, people he'd become friends with. All these connections were important to her.

When they entered the church, several people nodded at Gus. His hand pressed to her back he guided her toward a middle-aged couple standing near the back of the chapel. "Emily, I'd like you to meet Sam and Judy Parker. They've been very good to me since I moved here."

Smiling, they shook hands. Judy touched Emily's shoulder, her voice a whisper. "I'm so pleased that Gus has found someone. He had a very difficult time when Annabelle passed away."

"I can only imagine what it must have been like for him arrive home and find her," Emily offered, feeling a sudden connection to this woman.

Judy nodded sympathetically. "He was devastated. We didn't see him for weeks after. We called but he just didn't want to talk." She clutched Emily's hand. "He's a good man. He gives so much to the church, and I'm not just talking about money. He really cares about people."

"He *is* special," Emily said, smiling at this woman who said such nice things. "This is the first time I've met any of his friends. I've only been here a couple of weeks. I've learned that he's a very private person."

"Well, we'd all like to get to know you. Would you like to join the weekly Bible study group? I'd be more than happy to pick you up, save you driving here until you get to know the city better."

"I don't know. I have to confess that I haven't gone to church for years. And after my husband died, I didn't feel the need... Couldn't seem to get back to it," she said, apologetically.

"That's okay. We also have a Willing Sisters Sewing circle where we knit baby blankets for the newborn babies in the hospital. We also put together hospital packages of things a new mother would need; diapers, baby bottles, things like that. Would you be interested in that?"

"I haven't sewn or knitted anything in years, but I'd love to get back to it." Emily smiled in relief. She had found something in common with this woman, something they could hopefully build a friendship on. "I'd love to be part of your group."

"Then, it's settled. I'll pick you up this Wednesday around eleven. We have lunch while we're here. I'll bring our lunch this week, and you can bring our lunch next week," Judy said, hugging Emily. "We're going to have fun. I'm glad to meet you." She leaned closer. "I didn't know Gus had found anyone new, but I'm sure happy for him, and for you," she whispered.

All through the Anglican service, the old hymns she knew, the way Gus sang with enthusiasm, Emily felt really pleased. The priest, Gerry Green, was a wonderful speaker, his children's story making everyone in the congregation chuckle.

She glanced around the congregation, seeing so many pleasant faces, so much enthusiasm. These people were kind and thoughtful, and she wanted to be involved any way she could. She understood why Gus was a part of this church. She'd be sure to volunteer for a committee, which would give her even more contacts within the church. She smiled up at Gus. He winked at her.

Things were going to be just fine. She could feel it in her bones. These were good people. She and Gus were going to be very happy amongst these people. She'd just have to curb her imagination and not let it get the better of her. As the collection plate was passed, Emily felt a sense of contentment that had eluded her since Mark's passing.

CHAPTER SEVEN

The next morning, Emily had just put a pan of muffins in the oven when Gus appeared behind her, wrapping his arms around her and kissing her neck.

"Okay, honey, I have to be at the shelter for a couple of hours, then drop some things off at the dry cleaners. Is there anything I can get you while I'm out?" Gus asked, as he brushed past her and poured a cup of coffee for himself.

"You're going to have something to eat before you leave?" She raised a questioning eyebrow at him. "I'm baking muffins and I made pancakes," she said, taking the plate out of the warming oven.

"You are baking up a storm. This is great. I've barely used this kitchen in the past few years. Never seemed to have time. I'd love pancakes, and I'll have muffins tomorrow morning," he said, sliding into a stool on the other side of the island.

She passed him a plate, and the maple syrup. "I'm sure you'll like these. Grace and Mark insisted that I make them at least one weekend a month." She saw a look on his face, something odd about his expression. Had she upset him?

"Sorry. I didn't mean to bring that up. We're in a new life together now."

"No. It's okay. We both have memories of our spouses and our families. How's Grace, by the way?"

"She's busy. I tried to call her a bit ago when I was out with Jasmine and I woke her up. Forgot the time change, an hour and a half."

"Yes, I suppose that's a bit of adjustment you'll both have to make. Maybe it would be easier if you set aside a certain time each day."

"Won't work with her schedule, court and all. But we'll always find time to talk."

"Yes, you're really close."

"She's my only child. I love her very much."

He reached across the island, taking her hand in his. "And I love you. Whatever makes you happy, makes me happy."

"I really enjoyed meeting Judy and Sam yesterday," she said. "She's picking me up to go to the sewing circle she's part of on Wednesday. I think I may see if I can volunteer at the church."

"Why would you want to do that?"

"Well, you're very involved in your volunteer work. I'd like to be too."

"Don't rush into anything for now. We need to pay attention to us, to our life together."

"I'd like that too. But, to be honest, I often feel left out of parts of your life."

His eyes held hers, a small frown forming, his lips working. "What do you mean?"

"You're out a lot with your volunteer work at the shelter. You spend a lot of time in your office. I realize it's your space, and you were doing all these things before I came here. But I don't have anything of my own yet in St. John's, and that leaves me feeling a little lost at times."

He gave her a wan smile. "I'm glad you mentioned this to me. I wasn't aware I was neglecting you, leaving you alone so often. After Annabelle died I guess I let my volunteer work fill my life. Tell you what, I'm going to change things from here on. I'll let the people at the shelter know that I have to cut my hours back, and I'll be here for you."

"That would be really nice," Emily said, as a tiny voice in her head wondered why he hadn't realized this on his own.

After Gus left, Emily felt a little forlorn. It wasn't that she didn't enjoy his home, or having Jasmine to care for: it was being alone, so far from home, from everything familiar.

As she placed the pan of muffins on the cooling rack she wondered why she hadn't anticipated how lonely she might be here. "I guess that's love," she said to the quiet space, the only acknowledgement being Jasmine's groan from her dog bed.

She had had no idea how busy Gus's life was before she got there, something that hadn't occurred to her. He was supposed to be retired. He'd never talked about the hours he spent at the shelter, or the work he did for his church. Were there other parts of his life she didn't know about?

Yet, he had promised to change that part of his life, and she would accept that he'd do his best. After all, Gus was such a kind person, and someone who had struggled to get over the loss of his wife. She'd keep that in mind, as they worked things out between them. Living together meant they'd both have to give a little, make adjustments to accommodate their differences.

Once the kitchen was cleaned up, Emily decided that she'd see if the camera was where Gus had left it. She hoped he'd taken it away, and maybe he had. In the living room, she searched the top shelf and found the camera tucked in next to an ugly figurine. Her heart sank.

Why didn't he remove it? He knows I'm not comfortable with it being here, doesn't he?

For some reason her mind went to the day he'd given her the new phone, a hint of condescension in his tone, suggesting to her that she wasn't good at technology. And she wasn't. But maybe she could focus on learning more about all this tech stuff that Gus took for granted.

And despite being annoyed that he'd left the camera there, she could use it as a place to start learning about technology. She'd prove that she could be just as smart about all this stuff as he was. Well, maybe not just as smart, but still...

She got on her iPad, searched for the unit by name and found a picture that looked just like the camera on the shelf. It would seem the unit was capable of sending a signal to a computer that would record continuously to something called the Cloud. She made notes as she read. She began to understand a little of it, and as she continued to read she wanted to know more.

Having read all the information she could find, she decided to search the local electronics stores in St. John's for the same brand name of the camera and found a dealer in the main mall downtown. A company called Smithtech. They were open and that meant she could go and talk to someone about the camera.

Later, she was pleased and surprised at how easily she found the mall. She parked and went inside, only to discover that the store she wanted was just inside the entrance she'd used. Feeling emboldened, she entered the store and was greeted by a middle-aged man with a wide smile.

"I'm Lance Smith. Is there something I can do for you today?"

"I need your help," she said, pulling a piece of paper out of her purse. "This is information about a camera. Can you tell me how this works?"

He turned the paper over in his hand. "I've only installed these particular cameras in one house. Where did you get this?" he asked carefully.

"Oh. I'm living at Gus Parsons house. I mean, we're in a relationship. And I found this camera in his living room." She saw the look of surprise on his face. "I didn't go looking for it. It was on a shelf in the living room. I...I'm not good at tech things, and I'd like to learn more. I mean, I'd like to know about how this works, and what the Cloud does. To be honest, I want to impress Gus with my knowledge of technical things. He's really tried to help me learn about high-tech things, but I'm a little embarrassed about what I don't know."

"Well, you've come to the right place. I'm the local distributor for this equipment and I installed this system for Gus along with his security system, back a few years ago, for the reason you've described. It's good solid technology, that records everything and stores it on the Cloud, which is a sort of universal storage place for digital material."

"Thank you for telling me. I hate to ask Gus this sort of question. Not that he isn't helpful – he is – but I want to prove that I can learn to manage these things on my own. Do you mind if I ask you a few questions about the keypad at the back entry?"

"You're living with Gus?"

"Yes. We're together."

"Okay. What do you want to know?"

"Gus puts his thumb on a keypad to open the door, and unlock the system. Theresa, his cleaning lady, uses a code. Is there more to the system?"

"From the point of view of setting up access, that's about

it. You either have your print in the system or the code or, in Gus's case, both."

"Gus told me about the cameras around the property that are triggered by movement."

"Again, all very common technology for keeping a property secure. He can access those cameras and the security system from his phone. He can lock or unlock the doors. He can even change the access code from his phone. Gus wanted the best. He spent a lot of money making his property completely secure. I'd even go so far as to say he has a bit of a fetish." His eyes assessed her for a moment. "Would you like to know more about the systems he installed? You'd be able to impress him with your knowledge. Gus would like that, I'd think."

"Sure. How do I find out?"

"There's a website... Do you have your cellphone with you? I could put the site in your favorites listing and you could look at it when you get home."

"I can do that on my cell phone?"

"What kind of phone do you have?"

"I have a new iPhone." She reached in her purse to show him. "Oh! Darn! I left it at home."

"That's okay. I'll write down the Internet address of the site and you can look at it when you get home."

"Thank you."

"You want to impress Gus with your tech knowledge?"

"Yeah. He's kind and patient about me not knowing things about phones and computers." She smiled in apology. "My husband and my daughter were my go-to tech people, which meant I never really learned anything about extras on my phone. My computer is ancient. In fact, I didn't bring it with me because I thought I could use Gus's computer. But he has such a huge set-up in his office."

"How do you get your email?"

"He gave me a new iPad when I arrived. It works really well for what I need."

He passed her his business card with the Internet site written on the back of it. "If I were you, I'd learn everything I could about your new iPad. And if you need help, come in here and I'll help you."

"That's kind of you. Gus is so busy, I hate to be asking him all these questions." She turned to go, then a thought occurred to her. "There is one thing. Why would Gus leave the camera there when he didn't need it anymore; or would it still be part of his indoor security system?"

"I don't think it was meant to be part of his security system, not that he'd told me. Maybe he simply forgot about it. It's probably turned off."

"How would I know?"

"It has a tiny, needle point red light showing on the bottom of it."

Had she missed that? "That's it?"

He nodded. "Like I said, if you need any help learning new things related to your iPad or the Internet, I'm here. My phone number's on my card."

Gus stared out the window of Penny's condo, anger rising inside him. Penny's behavior had to be contained. He'd watched the footage of her condo after their last argument, worried that she might take her anger out on Tessa. She hadn't that he could see, but Penny was dangerous when she was angry. He'd spent as much time as he dared away from Emily to the point where she was getting suspicious. A dangerous situation as far as he was concerned.

But Penny had been even more erratic and hateful with him since she'd moved to Newfoundland. He's always known she was high-strung, but since she'd been living in St. John's her behavior had gotten more difficult to manage.

"Gus, how much longer are you going to keep that bitch at the house? Last time you told me that you hadn't decided how we'd kill her. But I've been doing a little research on my own, and potassium chloride is quick and easy. We've never used that before."

"And we may not use it this time. It all depends."

"On what? You promised me she'd be a quick one. You'd kill her and no one would be the wiser. We'd do it together. Then I get some story from you about needing her money. But why? We've never spent this long on a kill before. What the hell is going on?"

"Like I said, this is going to take a little more time. The payout this time will be big enough for us to do anything we want."

"No!" Penny slammed her fist into the wall next to him. "I don't care about payout! I looked it up. We could use potassium and it would be over real quick. You're living out in the woods. No one can get on the property without you knowing. We could spend the evening watching it all happening, the way we always do."

"Penny, this one serious has money. I want that money. We need that money," he said, trying to keep his tone neutral, keep her from getting angrier. He didn't need this. Any of it.

"When did this become about money?" she screamed.

He grabbed her arms, slamming her into the wall, shaking her hard. "Stop it! You have got to get control. Stop it."

She writhed in his grip. "You're sleeping with her! You're spending time with her like you were serious. I put up with that over that bitch Annabelle, because I love you and she was too sick for you to play around with. And I wanted you to enjoy this whole thing as much as I do. But I'm not going to put up with this much longer. I have already found Cindy.

We could begin to work on her right away. I've had coffee with her, heard her whole tale of woe. She's as stupid as a brick. An easy victim. It's my turn. I want to do it. You promised me I'd get to do in the next one, only now you're playing house with...her!"

"I'm not sleeping with her. We're not sharing a bedroom. I gave her some story about not wanting to rush things."

"I don't believe you. She's your type. Well dressed. Attractive. Money. Gullible. Easy to manipulate."

"Believe me when I say this is about the job. Nothing more—"

He felt the buzzing on his chest where his cell phone was. He'd set it up to alarm to let him know whenever Emily left the house. "Hold on a minute."

"What?" Penny asked squirming out of his grip, rubbing her arms, a scowl etched on her face.

He checked the cameras, spotting his Audi pulling out of the garage. Emily at the wheel.

"Where the hell is she going?"

"So your little bitch bird is going to fly away from you. I warned you. She's got her own money, and she's used to getting what she wants."

"Be quiet. I have to track her," he said, accessing the tracker on her phone.

"Well, while you're playing your little surveillance game, I'm going to get a beer," Penny said, going into the kitchen.

Emily couldn't be going very far. "She said she didn't need anything picked up. She's probably just going for a drive out of boredom."

"You'd better hope." Penny kicked the fridge door closed.

He'd watch and see what she did, and then decide. He gave his wife a quick glance, remembering their conversation and the woman's determination to take part in a hurried removal – how he loved that term, one they'd invented over the years. They first used it during their days in British Columbia and later in Alberta.

Penny wanted to kill again. For him it was for the pure thrill of perfection in doing it without leaving a trace. For his wife, the actual killing was a compulsion; valuable but also unpredictable.

He couldn't blame her. It was what held them together – their thirst to commit the perfect murder – but in recent years something had begun to change between them.

He'd done two killings of women from the shelter. Solo. Lonely women who clung to his interest and concern. Women who believed him when he said he wanted them to have good lives away from the dangers they faced with the men in their lives. They'd been vulnerable and easy and he'd given them the perfect final resting place.

They were two transients hanging around the shelter, unremarkable in every way. Yet, he was drawn to them, drawn by something he couldn't identify in himself. He'd never experienced that before. He'd always been the one who did all the calculations, the planning. Penny had done that part in the beginning, but now she just wanted to kill.

He'd never thought this need to kill would become an obsession for him as it had for Penny. But in killing the two women, he had to face that fact that he enjoyed killing way too much. He had to contain it, had to slow the process down. And that was part of why he had been postponing Emily's death. He had to be sure he could control the impulse. If he couldn't control the impulse, he might slip up, make a mistake that would cost him dearly.

So far, though annoyed by her questions and expectations, he had succeeded in maintaining control. He wanted to keep it that way.

And there was something else.

His wife could not find out that he hadn't shared those

two killings with her. It wasn't that he hadn't wanted to share them, but with Penny you had to be very careful to control her. She would have insisted in being involved, and he knew she would hold him back from doing it quietly and quickly. She loved to kill. And if she did find out what he'd done, God only knew what she'd do. He didn't believe she would kill him, or at least not right away.

She knew his real vulnerability: Tessa.

He switched to the tracker on Emily's phone. He stared. It indicated that the phone was in the house. *What the hell!*

He went over to her iPad to check on any activity there. She'd been searching the Internet for information about the camera in the living room.

"Penny, I'm going to have to go."

"No," she said, holding a beer out to him. "I don't know what you do with the bitch, but you're not leaving here without doing your husbandly duty." She gave him a lewd grin.

Sighing inwardly, resigned to the fact that his wife wanted rough sex before he left, he fixed a smile on his face. "I always give you what you want," he said, taking the beer from her and downing it in one long swallow.

CHAPTER EIGHT

Emily drove slowly back to the house, her thoughts on what the man at the electronics store had said. There was no denying the impact of his words. Gus had left a camera on the shelf, even though the reason for keeping it there had passed. She wanted to believe that it was simply forgetfulness and the strain of grief, something she understood. But she simply wasn't sure, and being unsure of anything about Gus shook her to the core.

A part of her wanted to forget her conversation with the store owner. Yet, her first thought was to find the camera and see if it was on. And if it were true – that what she found hadn't been turned off or dismantled – how could she talk to Gus about that?

No matter how she brought it up, there would be things said that showed her distrust of him. But more importantly, if he'd left it on intentionally, that would damage her trust of him. And trust was so important, especially when she was about to give up the life she had in Boston for a life with him.

But what had her worried on top of everything else was this question: Why would he want to watch her when he wasn't there? And that's what he was doing if the camera was still on. Because the man had said, and she'd confirmed it on the Internet, that the camera would continuously record as long as the red light was on.

Her heart pounded. Her chest felt tight. If what she suspected *was* going on, she wouldn't be able to stay there. She couldn't trust him. Tears stung her eyes. She needed to talk to Grace.

She reached in her purse for her phone, then remembered she'd left her phone at the house. How could she have been so dumb as to do such a thing? What if she'd had a car accident? Her hands were shaking on the wheel as she turned into the driveway, speeding up as she approached the house.

There was only one thing she knew for sure. She had to check the camera and then find Gus. Find out what was going on with that camera. Depending on what he told her she could be out of there, headed for Boston, by this evening. Tapping the garage door button, she slowed and moved into her spot. Gus's car was already in the garage next to hers. The roar of the her car's powerful engine in the confined space filled her, forcing her to breathe over the dread pounding through her.

She got out, clutching her purse close to her as she made her way to the door. When she got there, it opened. Gus stood there, a look of fear on his face. "Where did you go? I've been worried sick."

"I went into town. I needed…to get out for a little bit." Holding her purse like a shield in front of her, she moved past him into the kitchen. "I forgot my phone."

"I know. I tried to call you, then found your phone here when I got back. What's going on?"

Gripping the counter, her knuckles shining white, she felt the sting as she bit down on her lip. "I'm sorry I worried you."

"You did, darling. I love you. I got home a bit ago, and

couldn't find you. I worry about you. Now tell me what's going on? Why did you suddenly need to go into town?"

She had to get to the living room, check for the camera. She had to know whether she was right or wrong. Everything depended on it. "I'll be right back," she said, heading into the living room, her eyes searching the top of the shelf.

She couldn't seem to see the camera, but maybe it was the light. It had been there this morning. Where would it have gone? She was still staring at the shelf when she felt the heat of his body, his breath on her neck.

"Emily, I'm sorry. Are you looking for the camera?"

"Yes. I thought I'd look at it."

"Why?"

"Because I needed to know more about technology, about the camera."

"Is that why you went into town?" he asked, his fingers playing along her neck.

"Yes. I didn't realize you hadn't removed the camera. I thought it odd, but I decided to look at it, see what I could learn about it. I got on the Internet and discovered that it records to the Cloud, whatever that means. I wanted to know more. I went to the local dealer and asked him about it."

"Why didn't you wait and ask me?"

She turned to face him, her cheeks warming. "Because for once I wanted to seem knowledgeable about computers and all that stuff. The technology. You and Grace know so much more than I do, and I wanted to see if I could learn. The man at the store was very helpful."

The last thing I need is Miss Dimples roaming around St. John's looking to satisfy her curiosity.

"And now you're back here wondering where the camera went?"

Embarrassed, but needing to tell the truth, to find out

what really was going on, she said, "Yes. It was here this morning."

"And you want to know why I didn't get rid of the camera after Annabelle died, right?"

She looked at him, saw the sincerity and concern in his eyes. Her first thought was to deny what he'd said, but if this relationship was going to work, she had to be truthful. "Yes. Why would you keep that camera up there on the shelf?"

"Because I'm not very bright. And sometimes I forget things." He took her hand in his and led her to the sofa. "As weird as it sounds, I'd forgotten that camera was there until you spotted it. I was embarrassed to admit that I'd over-looked it, left it there. As I said, it records to the Cloud, but the camera wasn't on. Never on after Annabelle passed away."

She could feel the tension drain away from her, could feel the fear in her mind ebb, and then relief flooded in. "I was worried that you'd left it on. That you recorded me, us."

"I would never do that to you, or to us. What goes on in this house is completely private. You have to believe me when I say that I only had the cameras because of my concern for my wife. When I got home today I felt really stupid that I'd left it there and so I removed it. And now I've worried you needlessly. I promise you, I took the camera away. It's no longer in this house." He touched her cheek. "You believe me, don't you?"

She looked into his eyes, at the sadness and…saw something else there she couldn't identify. "I do believe you. But Gus, we need to spend more time together. I feel really lonely out here away from everybody. I don't have friends, anybody to talk to. I find out that you have cameras in the house, surveillance and security covering the whole property and I feel…trapped."

Shit! First Penny and now this!

He took her hand, his fingers massaging her wrist, his eyes looking into the distance. "Emily, I never want you to feel that way. Ever. I want you to be happy here with me. But I would never try to stop you from going anywhere you want to go. You're not a prisoner here."

"I didn't mean it quite that way, and I realize now that I can get worked up over things I don't understand, like cameras and phones and—"

"And all the things I know about. It makes you want to be better at it, not to feel silly when you don't understand how something works."

"That's it. That's why, when I saw the camera still there, I looked it up on the Internet. I went into see Mr. Smith and he was very helpful. And by the way he really admires you. I could tell."

Someone else to deal with...

"And I like him, too. He's really good at what he does." He sighed and smiled. "Look, this hasn't been a good experience for either of us. What do you say we go into town, have a wonderful dinner and simply spend time together? And if you have any questions about anything, just ask."

"Anything?"

What now? "Anything."

"I would like to be involved in the women's shelter. I want to share your interests. I'm a nurse and I've raised a daughter. I know I could make a difference."

He stared at her with such intensity that she felt nervous and had to look away. "That's a good idea, Emily. Why don't we talk about it over dinner?"

"Are you serious?"

"Of course, I am. And if you get involved, maybe I'll have more free time. You see, all our resources go into staff who can counsel and help these girls and women manage their lives. They've been uprooted by an abusive partner and they need a lot of help. So, I think it would be great for you to get involved."

Emily hugged him, all the while vowing not to second guess everything Gus did. She had to stop doubting things, had to stop this needless worry. "I feel sometimes as if you are holding things back from me. I came here to be with you, to be part of your life and your family. But I feel as if there's something you're not telling me."

He shook his head slowly. Met her gaze. "There may be things...I don't know. It's all new for me. Having someone in the house who wants to be involved, who is not held back by illness." He gently touched her cheek, his fingers a caress. "But I'm going to try harder. I'll arrange for you to be part of my work at the shelter. And please tell me when you feel this way. As you've probably guessed, sometimes I'm not that smart when it comes to knowing what's going on, even when it's pointed out to me. I've always had to be in charge, take control. Growing up I lived with my mother, seldom saw my father. I learned to keep my feelings to myself as my mom got upset so easily. And now my behavior's affecting you. I didn't want that to ever happen. I'll do better. I promise."

She laps up this bullshit talk straight out of the psychiatric hospital in British Columbia.

Her heart went out to him. Mark had not been very forthcoming about how he felt, hadn't talked much except about everyday things. After weeks of talking to Gus on Zoom, she knew he was willing to share things, yet she'd let her suspicious mind get the better of her.

"We both need to adjust to being together. After all, at sixty-three and sixty-eight, we are in danger of being set in our ways."

He laughed. "We can't let that happen. Ever."

"That's right. We've got to stay open to change, even when

it involves tech stuff," she said, taking his hand in hers. "I love you."

"I love you too... Thank you for understanding. I know I'm a little over the top about safety and security." He shrugged, his smile charming. "Promise me one thing, will you?"

"Sure."

"You won't leave the house again without your cell phone."

"I promise."

Later, they had a wonderful dinner at an Italian restaurant. They laughed and talked and enjoyed being together. The Tiramisu had just arrived at the table when Gus leaned toward her, his hand reaching for hers across the white linen tablecloth. "I want us to be together as a couple forever," he said, his eyes holding hers, heightening the moment between them.

"I do too." She felt his closeness, the warmth in his eyes drawing her in.

He looked away for a moment, and then back. "Emily, I realize we still have things to work out between us, and it will take time. But I've never been happier in my life. And this may sound like it's too soon, but I would like you to consider something."

"Okay..."

"I want to marry you. I have since the first time I met you on Zoom. But I also know that you don't want to rush things, and I know I've done some pretty dumb things since you got here. But I want you to be involved in all parts of my life. I'd like us to consider inviting Grace here for a week as soon as it can be arranged. I know she's got a heavy schedule, but she wants you to be happy. And we need to get to know each other. What do you think?"

She hadn't expected him to bring up marriage so soon, and that was probably her insecurity and her age. Marriage meant that two people had to learn to share, to adjust to each other's way of living. Not just for the occasional weekend or vacation, but living together every day of their lives. Yet, she'd thought about marriage many times over the weeks they'd been in touch, the weeks where she learned how much they had in common with each other. Gus was everything she could have asked for.

"I'm glad to hear you say you want to marry me. We talked about it, and I think both of us have been a little reluctant to take the conversation further, but yes, we need to plan our future."

"My thought exactly. We're not teenagers. We have so much we want to do, so many places we want to see together."

He smiled and she couldn't help smiling back. "And I would love to have Grace visit us. We could take a tour of Newfoundland while she's here, and bring Tessa and Penny along. We could spend time together, have barbecues here. I'm excited."

She missed the quick roll of his eyes.

"That would be really nice. Our girls need to get to know each other. And Grace will be delighted to meet Penny and Tessa. We'll be a family; you'll see," she said, wanting to reassure him.

The next day, although amazed at how much her life had changed in such a short time, Emily could think of nothing else but the possibility of marrying Gus. To celebrate she decided to go into town to pick up a few things for dinner.

She'd found a copy of her favorite Julia Child's cookbook among the cookbooks in the kitchen, and had decided to make Beef Wellington.

It was a complicated recipe but she was determined to pull it off. After all, Gus had told her she could do anything she wanted in the kitchen, buy anything she needed to feel at home in his house. And today she planned to do just that. She had a list of several different colanders, and cutting boards, along with a French press; all the things she needed to make the kitchen feel like hers.

Emily had gone online and found a kitchen supply store in the same mall where she'd found the electronics store. She was feeling more confident about finding her way around the city, meaning that today's trip in town would be more relaxed and pleasant.

When she finished shopping she planned to call Penny and ask her out for lunch. Gus was busy at the shelter this morning, something about a budget meeting. Before their conversation about getting married she would have been upset at being left on her own again. But she decided last night that she would use the free time to see if she could start a relationship with Penny. Something that would be essential when she and Gus got married. And they would be married, she was pretty sure.

After they'd gotten home from dinner last evening, they'd talked for hours. She'd learned about his mother's controlling behavior, how he often found ways to be away from her. That it had made him sad that he couldn't talk to his mother. With regret, he'd talked about all those years when they might have been closer, if he'd only tried a little harder.

She'd learned something important about Gus last evening. Whatever happened in his life, he worked to make it better. She liked and admired that about him.

As she pulled into the parking lot at the mall, she looked

forward to finding all the things she needed. Once inside the store, the sales clerk helped her find everything on her list and suggested that she look at some of the spatulas, and frying pans. Gus's kitchen was huge and she couldn't remember what he had for frying pans. She decided against purchasing one until she checked out his. With a bag filled with her purchases she returned to the car where the sun beating down on her was a welcome relief after the fog earlier that morning.

Settling into the seat, she called Penny's number only to have it go to voicemail. She left a message letting Penny know what she had in mind, hoping she sounded upbeat and welcoming. She couldn't say she was disappointed about not talking to Penny, but still she hoped to find some sort of common ground between them.

Suddenly her phone buzzed in her hand, startling her. "Hello?"

"Mom. Where are you?"

"I'm sitting in the parking lot at the mall."

"I've been trying to reach you, and your phone kept going to voicemail."

"I was on the phone."

"Who were you talking to for over an hour?"

"I wasn't talking that long. I left a message on Penny's phone, but that only took a couple of minutes."

"That's weird. I thought you had your phone issues solved with your new phone."

"I did too."

"I'm really concerned about this whole phone thing," Grace said.

"I am too. I'll mention it to Gus."

"I'm glad to hear that. How's your day going?" Grace asked.

"Good. Gus and I went out to dinner last night, had a wonderful time."

"That's good. But Mom, you don't sound good. Is everything okay?"

"Yes. Yes. I...I... Gus talked about getting married last night."

"Mom! When did marriage become a part of this? You're still getting to know each other."

"It just came up, I guess. But it feels so, I don't know, so right somehow. I'm not sure you can understand that. I'm not sure I understand it myself."

There was a short pause, during which Emily heard Grace speak to someone, then asked them to close her office door. "Mom, please don't do anything rash. I know you and Gus care about each other, and you want someone in your life."

"We're just talking about it. And he's told me we'll take our time, get a marriage contract drawn up, look after all that stuff."

"Mom, I'm not talking about money. I'm worried that you are being carried along here by the romance of it all. You know the swept away by love thing..."

"I'm too old for romance," Emily protested.

"This from the woman who has read every Nora Roberts book in print."

"I admit it. I love romance," Emily sighed.

"All I'm asking is that you don't make any commitment until I can come and visit."

"You'd do that? Gus suggested that the other night. Oh, I would be so happy if you could visit. You'll see what a lovely place this is. Gus has everything. I have an Audi that he gave me to drive. And a new phone, and a new iPad. If I mention anything he runs out and buys it. All the shopping I just did was on his credit card. Sorry,if this sounds like it's all about money, but he's very generous."

"Mom, I understand how exciting this if for you. And if a man granted me my every wish I'd be thrilled, too. It's just that I'd like to be with you, see how thing are in your life. You realize that if you decide to marry him, you would most likely be living there."

"I know."

"Speaking of that, have you given any thought to renting your house? I had a client in the other day. He's moving here. He's renting an apartment at the moment, but they're looking for a house."

"It hadn't crossed my mind. Just too much going on at the moment."

"So, I won't mention anything to him…?"

"Gus and I still have lots to work out – where we would live being one of those things. And I want to be able to come to Boston, you know, go home when I need to. Maybe later when things get sorted out here."

"Mom, I can understand why you're not sure about this. I'm guessing you're not ready to make a major decision of any kind right now."

"That's true. And that's why I came here. To see if Gus and I have a future together. And I think we do."

"Mom, I know we've had disagreements over Gus. But I love you and want you to be happy. And if he's the one, that's fine by me. But maybe you should wait until I get there to do any more planning. What do you think?"

"I… This is all different, new to me. A few months ago, I was lonely and a little afraid of what my life would be like as time went along. Now, I have a chance at a new life with a man I love. I don't want to miss out on being happy."

"I don't want you to either, Mom. And I'm going to see if I

can move my schedule around and come to Newfoundland to see you and Gus."

"I would love that, Grace. Really. It would be wonderful to have you here with me, with us," Emily said, feeling a rush of tears, tears of loneliness for her daughter.

"Okay. I have to go, but we'll make plans. Love you, Mom."

"Love you, too."

After she hung up, Emily sat there thinking about what her daughter said. She was thrilled that her daughter was coming to Newfoundland. She would talk to Gus about it. He'd be pleased. She started the car and pulled out of the parking lot. She'd go to the shelter and talk to him. Maybe they could go to lunch to celebrate her news.

And thinking over what she and Grace talked about – returning to Boston. To her home. She realized that home was where the heart was. And more and more her heart was with Gus.

Happiness rushed through her as she eased into the traffic. When she got to the shelter she parked her car and went in. A young woman sat at the desk, a pleasant expression on her face.

"How can I help you?"

"I'm looking for Gus Parsons. He's here at a budget meeting."

The girl gave her a blank look. "No. He isn't here. I haven't seen him today. Are you sure he was supposed to be here?"

CHAPTER NINE

A ll the way home the girl's words rang in her head. Over and over. Gus wasn't there, hadn't been there all day. A horrible sinking feeling trapped her, jumbling her thoughts.

Emily tried to stay calm, to remember what she'd promised herself. She would not jump to conclusions about anything. Maybe Gus had tried to call her, to tell her his meeting had been cancelled. She checked voicemail but there were no messages. Each time she keyed in his cellphone it went to voicemail. On the last call she left a message.

She was so worried and preoccupied she nearly missed the turn into the driveway, and her last-minute maneuver had her wheels spinning on the soft edge, startling her out of her thoughts.

This had to stop. She could not continue to feel this way. Suspicious. Not able to find him when she needed to talk to him. She hated to think this way, but a pattern was beginning to form. She'd be upset and he'd have an explanation that left her feeling as if she'd simply misunderstood or made a mistake. She couldn't go on this way; one minute trusting him completely and the next feeling something was amiss.

She'd have it out with him when she got home.

As she pulled into the garage, Gus stood waiting at the door to the house. "There's something wrong with your phone. I've been trying to call you for over an hour. Where were you?" he asked, his words rushed and anxious.

She hadn't thought of it, but maybe Gus was developing a memory problem. "I told you I was going into the mall to get a few things for the kitchen. Don't you remember?"

He gave her an embarrassed glance, his shoulders slumped. "I do remember. It's just that I got home and you weren't here." He took her parcels from her. "But there has to be something wrong with your phone. I couldn't leave a message. I wanted to tell you that my budget meeting was cancelled, and that I had to go to the bank and deposit money for them. I'm not supposed to do that, put my own money in the account, but it's payday this Friday. Their finances are such a mess. Sometimes I wonder what I'm doing there. Really."

Relief slid through her. There wasn't a problem, none at all. "My phone's been acting up. Grace tried to call me, and couldn't get through. You tried to call me and couldn't get through. What's going on? This phone is new. It should be working even better than my old one."

It is. It's working just the way I set it up. You leave the house. I check who's calling.

"But I have great news. Grace did get through finally and she's coming to visit."

What! "That's great. When?"

"She's checking her schedule to see, but it should be soon. I told her we'd talked about getting married, and she wants to meet Penny, visit with us, get to know what it's like here. I mean if we're going to get married, we need to get our girls together, don't you think?"

Damn!

"We don't have to live here, if you don't want to. I'll live wherever you want to live."

"That's so sweet," she said, hugging him. "I guess we really hadn't talked about where we'd live. I'd assumed...here."

"No. Not at all. Penny is doing better in her job. Tessa is in a really good daycare. They are settling in much better in the past few weeks. As you know, I've been worried about her, but it's getting better."

"That's great. I left a message on her phone about lunch. I'll follow up with her. I really do want to spend time with her and Tessa."

Got to distract her... Something she's been asking for.

"Emily, now that we're both home here, and given that I've been really busy with my work, I want to show you some things in my office."

"Your office?" she said, surprised.

"I know. I've made a big deal out of keeping my office door closed, not inviting you down to see where I work."

"But you showed me your security system. Is there more?"

"A lot more. After talking about getting married, I want you to be knowledgeable about how things in this house work, and they're all controlled by computers. And I want to show you were I keep all the information about this house. It's going to be yours soon, and if anything happened to me—"

"Don't say that, please," Emily pleaded.

"I didn't mean it that way. Only that you need to learn everything. Come with me," he said, taking her hand and leading her down the stairs.

The first time down here with him, she hadn't noticed

that the office was at the end of a long corridor that had several turns in it, leaving Emily with no sense of direction or where she was under the house. "Have you always had your office down here?" she asked, feeling a little claustrophobic as the corridor seemed to narrow as they got closer to his office.

"I put this in when Annabelle was ill. I needed to have a space where I wouldn't disturb her." He opened the door. "It's completely sound proofed. Sometimes when Annabelle wasn't feeling well, and I had to work, I'd be able to use cameras like the one I showed you to keep an eye on her when I was down here. You'll be able to reach me from any part of the house, once I show you how the intercom works."

"You had a lot to manage with Annabelle sick here in the house, and you taking care of her," she said.

"It was a very difficult time," he said, and she heard the catch in his voice. She knew only too well what it felt like to have someone you love die and not to be able to do anything about it. She took his hand. "I understand. Been there."

"You have no idea what it means to me to have you in my life, to have someone like you who understands what I've lived through." He glanced around. "And that's why I wanted you to see how things work down here. I'm very proud of all this, and it's all meant to keep you and me safe. I know I'm a little obsessed with security, but in my line of work..." He shrugged and went to the huge table with four different computer monitors, each showing different things. One showed the CBC news channel. One showed the stock market. Two showed various parts of the property.

"What is all this? I don't remember seeing this before," she told him, her mind trying to adjust to the video showing the secret garden she loved. Had he been watching her when she was alone in the garden? *Stop doing this to yourself!*

He rested his hands on her shoulders, his touch warm and soothing. "Remember Mr. Smith at the electronics shop? He did this for me. He installed all the cameras, all the cables and Internet access, all the motion-detectors. I'm not trying to frighten you with all this. And I promise I don't ever check these cameras unless an alarm sounds here." He pointed to the bottom of a screen. "It's all linked to my phone so I can see anything that happens. I realize this sounds a little paranoid, I want us to be happy and safe, wherever we live."

"Why do you worry about safety?" she asked, as the smiled faded from his face. "I don't mean to be critical in any way, but did something happen to make you feel you weren't safe? That you had to go to these lengths?"

All it would take is sudden pressure on your neck...

"I grew up not feeling safe. But I searched for and learned things I could do that made me feel secure. And I want you to see how safe you are here. I have a backup generator for all this so it will never fail. I did this after I moved here because I realized that living in such a remote area, with lots of trees on the property, it would be easy for someone to break in. Annabelle didn't worry about such things. She seldom locked her doors, for God's sake," he muttered.

"And being in the surveillance business you couldn't live like that," she said, seeing the dark glint in his eyes. She turned in his arms, bringing her hands to rest on his where they rested on her shoulders, holding her fast.

He twitched. "Well, my business wasn't just surveillance," he said, his tone shadowed with annoyance.

Was he a little defensive over what he'd done for a living? "Sorry. But that is the business you were in before you sold. And you still work for your old company when you're asked, right?"

"On occasion," he said, his tone firm.

"I'm proud of you, of your success. And that you've done all this to keep your home, our home, safe. I can't imagine what this would have cost, or how long it took to install."

"It was quite complicated," he said, brushing his hands over her hair, his fingers coming to rest on her cheek.

"Show me how it works. How do I switch from one camera to another?" she asked, sliding into the chair in front of the screens.

Killing her would be such a release. Such a thrill.

"See this?" He sat in the chair next to her. "You just do this, and it will give you a different camera."

"Slow down!" she said, touching his hand on the keyboard. "I can't keep track of what you're doing if you don't wait for me. Remember I'm not a computer person, but I want to learn."

And she did. She sat with him while he showed her how it worked, sometimes speaking faster than she could comprehend. "Slow down!" she teased. "I'm not as good at this as you are."

"Sorry!" His jaw worked as his hands slowed over the keys. He took his time showing her how to access the Cloud. He went back in the footage and showed her the day she first went into the garden along the drive.

Suddenly it all began to make sense, how the cameras moved, going from one camera to another. And there was a menu with choices... "What does 'back up to the Cloud' mean?"

"It's storage of all the data on these cameras. Like your computer at home."

She didn't know anything about that, but she focused hard on what he was showing her, determined to memorize the steps. "That's amazing. I don't know if I can remember all the steps, but I'm going to try."

"I'm sure you'll get the hang of it."

She stared at the screen showing where she sat in the garden. "I look terrible, don't I? If you're upgrading this again, get a camera that makes me look less like an old woman."

"You'll never be old to me," he said. *You're not going to live long enough.*

"That's sweet." She glanced around. "Such a huge space. A file area? A door? Where does that go?"

"It's another way out of the house in case of a fire."

"Where are we? I mean we're under the house, but what part of the house?"

A part you'll never know about. "Out near the front of the house, near the septic field."

"The what?"

"It's where all the stuff from the sinks and toilets go to be composted. A little complicated, and not used in cities."

"We once had a cottage that had a septic field, something Mark looked after. He hired someone to come in and look after it. Once it backed up on us, and a truck came to clean it out. They called the truck the 'honey dipper,'" she said, smiling as she moved closer to look at the screen.

Death by mundane shit. Pun intended. No fear. Brainless is here.

"Let's leave this for now. You must be bored looking at all this, and you can always ask me questions later if you want to," Gus said.

"Sure. I've got a wonderful dinner organized for us. I need to do a little more work to complete it, but maybe you can choose a wine?" she asked.

"What are we having?" he asked as they made their way back upstairs into the bright light of the kitchen.

"I'm making Beef Wellington."

"Wow! Is it a special occasion?" he asked, hugging her close, his fingers in her hair as he turned her in his arms and kissed her.

"Hmm... It could be. After all, we need to make plans for

Grace. I'd like to have Penny and Tessa here for dinner the day after she gets here."

"We could do that. Penny's often on call at the real estate firm but I'm sure she can arrange to have the night off."

He kissed her again, making her heart pound with need.

"I…I love you. We're going to be so happy," she whispered against his lips.

He held her at arm's length and looked into her eyes. "I have to ask you something."

"What's that?"

"Just a minute. I'll be right back."

He disappeared up the stairs and when he came back he was carrying a small black box. "I'm too old to get down on bended knee, but it doesn't change what I want to say. Emily Carling, will you marry me?" he asked, reaching for her hand.

"Oh! Oh!" She watched as he opened the tiny box and took out a very large diamond ring. It was the most incredible ring she'd ever seen. She was here with the man she loved, in the home they would share with each other. She'd felt blessed to have found him. She felt as if she'd known him for a very long time. He meant the world to her. And now he wanted to marry her.

"Yes. I'll marry you!" she said as he slipped it on her finger.

This ring has been useful so many times.

"I promise to marry you whenever you'd like to tie the knot." He grinned at her. "Just don't take too long. I'm getting up there in years, you know."

"You are not," she said, kissing him playfully, wrapping her arms around his neck and holding him close. He held her so tight she could barely breathe. She could feel his body shuddering against hers. "Hey. You're not crying, are you?" she said, her heart filled with tenderness and love.

More like laughing.

. . .

They had a beautiful dinner together, shared a bottle of wine. She'd been reminded all over again about what a wonderful, caring person Gus was – and so tender. They'd spent the rest of the night in the master bedroom, entwined in each other's arms.

When she awoke she felt a little confused. The room was clothed in darkness. She reached over, her fingers trailing along the smooth linen sheets, searching for him. She turned sleepily to look at the small digital clock on the armoire: 5:00 AM.

"Gus," she said, pulling the duvet around her body as she glanced toward the door. "Are you here, honey," she said, sitting up on the side of the bed and going into the bathroom. Still no sign of him. She headed to the stairs, calling his name as she went down to the kitchen. There was no one there. Jasmine stirred in her dog bed, then gave a soft grunt and went back to sleep.

Maybe he had to leave for some reason. She went to the back door to check in the garage. The security system was on. If he'd gone out, why would he put the system on?

Out of the corner of her eye she saw a light along the hall toward the stairs leading to the basement. Was he up working so early? she wondered as she headed down the stairs. The air was cool, slightly stuffy, and at the end of the corridor she couldn't tell if he was in the office or not as there was no light shining anywhere around the door. But where else could he be?

She turned the knob and the door opening soundlessly. "There you are, darling. I was wondering where you'd gone. Is everything okay?"

"What!" He turned to her, the screen in front of him going dark. "Don't sneak up on me like that!"

"I'm sorry. I didn't mean to. I woke up and you were gone." She crossed the room and wrapped her arms around his neck. "I missed you. Why are you up working at this hour?"

What did she see? Anything? My plan is almost ready... Only a few adjustments needed

"I came down here to work on my surprise for you."

He's trembling, she noticed. "What surprise?"

"I was looking for interesting places to honeymoon. Did you know there are all sorts of very lovely hideaway vacation spots for couples who want to get away from it all, to the privacy of their own beach, their own lovely cottage with wonderful sea breezes?" he said, hugging her tightly in his arms.

His smile was so wonderful. She would never tire of seeing his eyes light up when he talked to her. He was easily the most attentive man she'd ever known. "I've never looked, but I'm excited that you're looking."

"I want us to have the most beautiful honeymoon. I've marked all the sights I found, so the minute we have a wedding date, I can book it."

"I'll go wherever you want to go."

"Well, right now, I want to go back to bed with you, soon-to-be Mrs. Gus Parsons."

"I want that too," she said, happily as they headed for the stairs and their bedroom.

Later, Emily fell asleep, her head resting on Gus's shoulder.

Close call tonight. But I've found Emily's cause of death. Penny will be pleased.

CHAPTER TEN

The next morning, Emily got up, dressed and tiptoed downstairs. She planned to make them a wonderful breakfast in celebration. She'd make waffles with maple syrup, coffee in her new French press, and champagne. She'd get Gus to pick which champagne they'd have from his over-sized wine fridge. But first, she'd let Jasmine out in the back-yard for a few minutes while she got organized.

She was preparing the batter for the waffles when she heard Jasmine yipping to come back in. Once inside, Jasmine ate from her bowl before sitting down to watch Emily. Emily talked quietly to the dog whose bright eyes followed her everywhere she went in the kitchen. She'd grown very attached to Jasmine in the time she'd been there. The dog was such good company.

She was just setting the table with bright floral dishes she'd found in the cupboard when Gus appeared at the counter.

"Why didn't you wake me?" he asked, coming over to wrap his arms around her waist.

"I wanted you to sleep while I got breakfast, something

special to start our new life." She leaned back in his arms, inhaling the scent of him. "I've texted Grace to tell her I need to talk to her this morning. She texted back to say she'll be out of court in about two hours from now. I want you with me when I tell her about our plans."

"Sounds good to me," he whispered against her neck. "I'll let Jasmine out while you finish what you're doing."

"I already let her out for a few minutes. I'm going to walk her later." She smiled up into his eyes. "In the meantime, why don't you sit down? I'll bring the plates of waffles to the table," she said.

"I'll bring the coffee," he said, stepping around her as he reached for the carafe. "Oh, I'm looking forward to this coffee today. I've never had a French press," he said, smiling as he carried the carafe to the table.

As she sat down across from him, taking in his carefully combed hair, his impeccable shirt and tie, she marveled at how composed Gus always looked. "What a difference a day makes." She chuckled as she picked up her fork. "Such a cliché I realize, but true. Who could have imagined yesterday that today we'd be looking forward to our wedding?"

"It's true. Life can change in a heartbeat." He took a bite of the strawberry-covered waffle, smiling as he chewed. "Wow! This is delicious."

"Glad you like—"

Gus's phone made a trumpeting sound. "That's Penny." He scooped up his napkin. "Better answer that," he said, going to the counter for his phone. "Hello."

Emily heard a woman's voice yelling across the room. Gus held his phone away from his ear. He pointed and mouthed the word *Penny* before heading down the stairs toward his office.

Disappointed, her food untouched, Emily waited for Gus to return. When he did, he was very apologetic. "I'm sorry.

Penny needs to see me. She's bringing Tessa with her because she has the sniffles and isn't allowed to go to daycare."

"Maybe it would be better if Penny stayed home with her," Emily said, fighting to hide her irritation.

"Look, she needs to talk to me. I know you went out of your way for this lovely breakfast, so let's finish our breakfast before she arrives. What do you say?"

"Do I have a choice?"

He sat down across from her, an ingratiating smile on his face. "I know this isn't fair to you, but I can't say no to her."

"Well, Gus, you're going to have to learn because I'm not willing to have Penny behave as if she's in charge here. This is our home, our life – not hers." She snapped her napkin in place on her lap.

They ate the rest of their breakfast in silence. As she glanced across the table at him, she made up her mind. Gus needed to do something about Penny's behavior soon, if this relationship was going to work. "Did Penny say exactly what Tessa had? Is it a cold? The flu?"

He shrugged. "Don't know. We'll see, I guess."

About an hour later, Penny appeared at the door with Tessa. Tessa ran into Gus's arms, her mass of auburn curls bouncing around her head. A smile creasing his face, he picked her up and carried her into the living room, cooing and talking softly to her.

For a change Penny made eye contact with Emily. "I'm sorry I didn't return your message from the other day, but I've been busy. Things are sort of difficult for me right now."

Aren't they always? Emily kept quiet.

"Could I ask a favor?"

"Of course."

Penny fixed her gaze on Gus as he came back into the kitchen carrying Tessa. "Could you entertain Tessa while I talk to dad?" Penny asked. A smile flickered to life, but faded quickly.

Maybe caring for Tessa would make it easier to get a relationship started with Penny. "Sure. I'd like to get to know Tessa a little. What does she like to do?"

"The cartoon channel," Penny said, pushing the child in Penny's direction, before turning to Gus. "Can I talk to you downstairs?"

Once they were gone, Emily bent down to speak to Tessa. "Would you like to help me walk Jasmine?"

Tessa looked at her for a minute, her thumb in her mouth, her eyes darting from the hall where Penny and Gus had gone then back to Emily's face. Pursing her tiny lips, she nodded.

"That's good. I'll show you how to put the leash on Jasmine, and you can walk her. I'll be right beside you. We'll go down to the secret garden. Did you know your grandfather has a secret garden?"

Tessa frowned. "A secret? I know a secret," she said.

"Is your secret fun?"

Tessa shook her head until her auburn curls were swinging around her cheeks.

"Then, maybe you'll enjoy the secret garden because it'll be fun. Jasmine loves it. And it's got a lovely new bench. Why don't we take a picnic on our walk and eat it on the bench?"

Tessa smiled and clapped her hands.

"What would you like to take on a picnic?" Emily asked.

"Peanut butter. Mommy says I can't take peanut butter to school. I love peanut butter and crackers."

"Then, it's settled. We'll make a picnic and take Jasmine for a walk."

The walk down the driveway to the garden was pleasant with the sun sparkling through the trees. Jasmine held the leash in her tiny fingers as she talked to Jasmine. The dog walked along very quietly beside the little girl, and Emily followed, feeling very content despite Penny's behavior.

She checked her watch. Grace should be calling soon. She wanted to tell her daughter about their plan to marry, and that she wanted her to come to Newfoundland for the ceremony.

As they entered the garden, Tessa stopped. "Where are we going?"

"To the new bench, just a little farther along, just beyond the statue, in the other part of the garden," Emily said, taking Tessa's hand in hers.

Tessa stopped. "No! Don't go there!"

"Why?" Emily asked.

"Mommy says don't go there, down there between the trees."

Penny must have been concerned that her daughter would see the little grave stones, and ask questions. And maybe Tessa was old enough to remember one of the other dogs. "We don't have to go if you don't want."

"Can we go there?" she pointed to the other bench.

"Of course we can. I'll follow you," Emily said as they started along the path.

Once there, they sat down beside each other. "Can I have peanut butter and crackers now?" Tessa asked squinting up at Emily.

"You sure can. What should we do about Jasmine?" Emily asked, as the dog sat down next to Tessa. "I didn't bring any picnic for her."

"She can have some of mine," Tessa said, holding out a cracker to the dog.

"I don't know if she can have people food."

"I feed her people food when Mom isn't watching," Tessa said, bouncing on the bench as Jasmine tugged on the leash. Tessa gobbled her cracker, her eyes sparkling. "I'm going to let Jasmine off the leash," she said. She reached for the clip, her tiny fingers working quickly.

"I...I don't know if we should—" Jasmine gave a yip and raced for the entrance to the pet cemetery, then stopped and turned around.

Just then Emily's phone rang. She picked it up. "Grace?"

"Hi Mom, how's it going?"

"It's going really good. I'm in the garden with Tessa and Jasmine is off the leash."

"Do you need to catch her?"

"No. She's just sitting here watching us as we eat our peanut butter and crackers."

"The old Mom ploy. Get the child eating to keep them occupied."

"You remember that?"

"I do." Grace chuckled. "So you're babysitting Tessa. Where's Penny?"

"She and her father are talking."

"About what?"

"Something to do with her job, I think."

"That woman needs a shrink. She can't seem to cope with anything on her own."

"You may be right. I'm not sure."

"But you said yourself, she's very needy, very demanding of her father's attention."

"Yeah, she is." Emily sighed.

"What's going on? Your message sounded so excited. Are you making plans for my arrival? I'm booking off a few days next week, and I'm getting a flight organized."

"I can't wait to see you. You're going to really enjoy your time here. Gus is excited. He wants to show you around St. John's. And he asked me to marry him, and he's given me a diamond."

"He what!" Grace yelled.

"Yeah, can you believe it? He wants us to get married."

"But Mom you're just getting to know him, learn about his life. You have a lot of things to work out. I've listened to your uncertainties around Penny. You don't know anyone there yet."

"I met a lady at his church," Emily said, feeling a little defensive.

"And that's all good. It's just that you and Gus haven't had time to work out what life together will be like."

"That's true. But we've already talked about a marriage contract. He doesn't want anything of mine, and I don't want anything of his. And we talked about our wills. He's leaving everything to me."

"I don't believe that. What about Penny and Tessa?"

"They've been taken care of by his mother and father in their wills. They left Penny a small fortune when they passed."

"Do you believe him?" Grace asked, her voice rising. "Have you seen any of the paperwork around all of this?"

"No. We only talked it over last evening. Gus is going to get a lawyer to draw up the papers."

"Listen to me. This is going way too fast. I don't want you to sign anything until I get there. Do you hear me? Don't do anything without showing me the documents first."

"Grace, why are you so distrustful?"

"I'm in the business. Every day I see how women are taken advantage of because they believe what some man told them."

"I know, honey. But Gus isn't like that."

"How can you be certain?" Grace asked, her voice hard.

As usual, Emily had to wait for Grace to respond.

As she kept the phone to her ear, the sun warmed Emily's neck, Jasmine got up and ambled off toward the pet cemetery. Tessa leaned against Emily, her head nodding against her arm.

"Mom, I'm really worried for you. I don't know why suddenly there is this rush to get married. You really don't know very much about Gus. Did you ever look him up online? Did you ever check to see whether he was on LinkedIn? Many professionals and business owners are there. And what about his business? What do you know about it?"

Oh, she didn't want to have this discussion or an argument with her daughter. "Grace, I understand your concern. I will not sign anything until you've seen all of it. And besides, we're months away from making those kinds of decisions."

"I hope so," Grace said, followed by a long sigh.

Suddenly Jasmine was barking loudly. Tessa sat up, her eyes wide.

"Hold on a minute. I've got to see what the dog is doing. I hope she hasn't cornered a skunk."

"I'll wait," Grace said.

Holding the phone, Emily walked quickly down through the shrubs toward the lower garden toward the pet cemetery.

"Wait for me," Tessa said, running to catch up.

They entered the space together, to find Jasmine pulling on what looked like a piece of cloth. "What's that?" Emily grabbed Jasmine. The dog dropped the fabric at her feet.

Emily picked it up, feeling the softness of it in her hands. It had a beautiful floral pattern, with a tag showing an expensive designer's insignia. "I've just found what looks like a silk scarf," she said to Grace.

"What's it doing in the garden?"

"I have no idea. Someone must have left it here. This was Annabelle's favorite place. She must have been the one who dropped it."

But despite offering reassurance to her daughter, Emily felt a chill go down her spine as she glanced around. Why would there be an expensive scarf in the debris on the ground near one of the headstones? Whatever was going on, she didn't want to worry her daughter. "I'll check with Gus. He'll know whose scarf it is."

"That makes sense," Grace offered.

"I need to get Jasmine back on her lead, and get back to the house. Penny should be done talking to her dad, and is probably waiting for us. I'll talk to you later. And dear, I am pleased to hear that you're making plans to visit."

"I want you to be sure that you keep me in the loop about your plans. Remember, you're not to do anything involving legal things without telling me first. Okay?"

"I promise. And dear, I would never sign anything without running it past you first. You don't have to worry about that. Just be happy for me."

"Okay, Mom. I love you. Talk later."

Emily stared at the fragile bit of dirty silk in her hands, her mind tumbling over the possibilities. "Time to go," she said to Tessa as she clipped the leash on Jasmine and started for the house.

Penny grabbed her purse, her face flushed with rage. "I'm telling you now, Gus, that if she isn't dead the day after tomorrow, I am going to kill her myself."

"Don't be ridiculous. We will not ruin this thing we've got going. It's too important to both of us. Control your urges. We've enjoyed every minute of this life, and now we have the added advantage of another woman who has money. And with a little effort that money can be ours."

"Yeah. Yeah. I hear ya. But I'm done waiting around."

"No. You're not. I am going to get Emily to sign a few

documents that will make sure that her money is mine. Just like Annabelle. Think about it. If we do this right we'll be wealthy. We could even retire. We could live wherever we wanted once I'm done with Emily."

Penny struck his chest, forcing him back against the counter in the kitchen. "Do not think for one minute that we are going to stop. You can't stop. You love planning each death. We do it together and then have sex. You tape their deaths and we watch them over and over. You told me just today that last night you watched the video where we suffocated Annabelle. You called me after and I came in through the basement door." She clawed his chest, her nails digging into his flesh. "That Emily bitch didn't even know I was here. For God's sake! You can't give that up!"

He had to control his impulse to keep watching the videos. That's what happened after he killed the two strays from the shelter. He'd watched one of the videos and then went to the shelter. The thrill of those two young women, the secret life he'd started away from his wife when he killed them and buried them in the garden, made him ache for more.

"Penny, for the last time, I'm in charge. This is my victim. I will decide when she dies. Just like you did with Annabelle. Remember it was me who had to move on her, to woo her, and let you watch everything that was going on, just as now. Your choice was brilliant, and we profited by it. We will enjoy every minute of another well-planned kill. Let's stop talking about this before Emily gets suspicious."

"If I ever find out that you are having sex with her, I will kill you." She grabbed his shirt, shaking him. "You will not betray me that way."

He took her by the throat, squeezing until he saw raw fear in her eyes. "Enough! You've got to leave. If I'm going to finish our plan, I need to convince Emily to do a new will, to do a marriage contract. She has to believe that I am not after her money. Go home. Take Tessa and calm down." He let go of her.

Gasping she clutched the edge of the counter. "Don't you ever do that again," she croaked, tears welling up in her eyes.

Suddenly the back door opened and Tessa came in, her fingers wrapped up in Jasmine's leash. "Mommy!" she cried, racing to Penny and wrapping her arms around her legs. "Are you crying?"

Penny continued to sob, her knuckles white where she gripped the counter's edge.

"Oh! Penny! What happened?" Emily asked, rushing over to her.

Penny stepped back. "Nothing."

"She just got word a dear friend of hers died." Gus put his arm around Penny, squeezing her shoulder hard enough to make her wince. "She needs to get home, don't you Penny?"

Penny swallowed hard, her eyes wild as she stared at him. "I...I...Yes."

"Would you like us to keep Tessa? Give you a little time to yourself?" Emily asked.

"No." She grabbed Tessa's hand, yanking her along with her. "We're going," she said, stepping around Emily and heading for the door.

"Drive carefully, dear," Gus said. "Call me when you get home."

Emily watched as Gus followed Penny out through the garage to the driveway, her mind on the stress she'd seen in Penny's eyes. There was a lot more going on here than simply being upset. There had been real fear in the woman's eyes. *Why would that be?*

In her experience, few people's first response to a death

was fear. Usually they were very sad, wanting to know why someone had died. Not looking as if she was afraid of something. But Penny was definitely different, with over the top reactions to so many things. Several times she'd tried to get Gus to tell her more about Penny, but he'd resisted. She wished she could get Gus to level with her about his daughter.

She went to take her jacket off and found the dirty silk scarf in her pocket. She'd nearly forgotten about it after the odd scene she'd witnessed a few minutes earlier. Turning it over in her hands, she spotted what looked like a brownish stain. It must have come from the dirt she found it in. She was looking intently at it when Gus came back in the door.

"Well, I'm sorry to see Penny upset like that. She takes things so hard. I wish she would simply concentrate on Tessa and her job, but I guess we don't—" He stopped. His expression froze.

"What's that?"

"I found it in the pet cemetery. It's a silk scarf. Jasmine must have dug it up. Whose is it?" She glanced at Gus.

His breathing was labored. His eyes radiated fear.

"What's wrong, Gus?" she asked, reaching for him.

He stumbled into the counter, his body shaking. "Call an ambulance. I think I'm having a heart attack!"

CHAPTER ELEVEN

S he managed to get Gus over to the sofa. His breathing was rapid, his pulse weak. The 911 call seemed to take forever, then finally a female voice answered. "911. What's your emergency?"

"I need an ambulance," she said, giving the address she'd memorized months before.

The emergency operator said that an ambulance was on the way. Relieved, yet frightened, Emily watched Gus, his skin color was pale, his eyes filled with fear. She couldn't lose him, not when they were finally together. "Gus, darling. I love you. You're going to be all right." She took his hand, her fingers seeking his pulse along his wrist. "The ambulance will be here soon." She had to believe that. He couldn't die on her, not now, not when they had everything to live for. "We'll need your health card and a list of your meds," she said, keeping her voice even.

"In my wallet," he gasped, clutching his chest.

She found it easily. "I'll stay right here with you until they arrive." She checked her watch. Took his pulse again, the beat even faster than the last time.

"Get Penny. I need Penny," he said, his voice rising.

"I'll call her, Gus, but you have to be calm."

"I have to talk to Penny!" He tried to sit up, but fell back against the sofa.

"Don't. Please stay calm. You need to stay calm," she repeated.

In the distance she heard the wail of sirens. "Gus, they're nearly here. I'm going to open the door."

He grabbed her hand, squeezing her fingers so hard she cried out.

"Don't leave me!" he rasped, his eyes wild.

"I won't. I'll follow the ambulance into the city. But right now, you need to calm down."

There was a knock at the door. She answered it. Two men came in, carrying a stretcher and two large black bags. They promptly began hooking Gus up to a portable ECG machine that beeped and whirred. One man took Gus's blood pressure, did a quick physical exam while the other asked Gus questions, reassured him that he was being cared for, that they would be transporting him to the hospital in a few minutes.

Relieved, Emily searched for her purse. She'd need it when she followed the ambulance to the hospital. When they got Gus onto the stretcher and out the door, she set the alarm and followed them.

The drive to the hospital was a very anxious trip, due in part to the fact that she found herself several trucks and a car behind the ambulance and missed the turn they took. When she finally arrived, they asked her to wait in the waiting room off the trauma area.

It was in that moment of quiet that she remembered she hadn't called Penny. Finding his daughter's number on her phone, she dialed.

"Yes." Penny's voice was harsh.

"Penny, it's Emily. Gus is in the hospital."

"What!" she screamed, the sound filling the air.

"Penny, your father had some sort of spell. They brought him to emergency. I'm in the waiting room."

"I want to talk to the doctor, now!" Penny yelled, forcing Emily to move the phone away from her ear.

"They haven't come out from the trauma room yet."

"I'll be right there," she said, her tone strained.

The line went dead and that was such a relief. It was becoming increasingly difficult to be around Penny when she was upset.

Really, Penny was the least of her worries. Gus hadn't looked good when they put him on the stretcher. She knew from her nursing experience that they would monitor him, take more blood for testing, and order various other tests to determine the cause of his sudden attack.

As she sat there she was suddenly overwhelmed with anxiety. She needed to talk to Gus. She needed to see him. To know he was okay. Dialing Grace's number, she waited nervously to hear her daughter's voice, the reassurance of knowing that Grace would be calm and capable; she needed both right now.

"Hi Mom."

"Gus is in the hospital. He had some sort of spell this morning," she said, sobbing in relief at hearing her daughter's voice.

"Mom. Where are you?"

"I'm in the waiting room. They're supposed to come out and talk to me."

"Where's Penny?"

"She's on her way here. I think this all started because Penny was terribly upset this morning. A friend of hers died and her father couldn't seem to calm her down. He's always so concerned for her."

"I'm more worried about you. Are you okay?"

"I don't know." She tried to swallow over the lump in her throat. "I had something happen this morning, and now I'm really worried about Gus. He didn't look good. The ambulance came quickly. A huge relief."

"What happened to you, Mom?"

She glanced toward the door, half expecting Penny to appear. "I had Tessa out for a walk. We went to the pet cemetery to the bench near there. Remember? I told you about the silk scarf half-buried in the dirt that I found."

"Yes. But what does that have to do with anything?"

"Gus and Annabelle had a special burial place for their pets. Tessa and I were there this morning," Emily said, her voice shaking. "It's been stressful."

"Mom, do you realize how bizarre that sounds? What is going on there? What did Gus say when you told him about the scarf?"

"When I got back to the house Penny was still upset, and Gus was trying to calm her. Then when she left I showed him the scarf but didn't get a chance to tell him much. He started having pain and I had to call the ambulance."

"Mom, I think you should come home. Something's not right over there."

"I can't leave Gus. He's ill. He needs me."

"Mom, you're not responsible for him."

"But I am. I'm going to marry him. I can't just walk out."

"Mom, I didn't want to tell you this right now. I was going to wait until I got over there to check it out for myself."

"What are you talking about?"

"Mom, I contacted your cell phone provider. They have complete cell phone coverage in the area of Gus's house. There is no reason you should have had cell phone problems, and therefore no reason why you needed a new cell phone. Why would Gus insist that you have a new phone?"

"Grace, I can't think about that right now. Let's talk about it later. Penny just arrived, and I have to go."

Once she saw the frantic look on Penny's face Emily hung up and moved toward her.

"Penny, the doctor hasn't said anything yet. How are you doing?"

"You did this, didn't you?"

"What?"

"Gus was fine when I left. You're a nurse. You'd know what to do to hurt him."

"Penny! That's enough! You're upset, but you're talking crazy. Stop it!"

"You stop it. You get out of here. I'll look after him. You're not needed here."

Emily gritted her teeth. "I'm staying right here until we hear from the doctor."

Like two prize fighters they went to separate corners of the waiting room. Emily refused to look at Penny. She'd had her fill of the woman. For Penny's part she sat glaring at the door.

Finally, the doctor arrived. They rushed to him, Emily spotting the name tag: Dr. Leigh. "Is Gus okay?" Emily asked.

"I'm his daughter. I have his power of attorney." Penny pushed in between Dr. Leigh and Emily.

Looking surprised, the doctor directed his remarks to Penny. "Your father is stable. We haven't found any sign of a heart attack yet, but we will keep him in for a few days for testing. He's going to intensive care right now. You'll be able to visit him in about an hour."

Penny gave a dissatisfied sigh, a hard scowl forming on her face.

"I'll speak to you tomorrow," Dr. Leigh said, clearly happy to be leaving the room.

Emily didn't know what to do. She didn't want a confrontation at Gus's bedside, and she didn't want to spend any more time around this woman. "Penny, I'll go back to the house, check on Jasmine and make sure things are okay."

"You're leaving! You really don't care, do you? You just want his money. Is that it?"

Emily had had enough. "Penny, you're upset. I'm upset. You seem to feel I have no place here. I just thought I'd go back to the house while you speak to your father alone. I'll come back later and sit with him. Tessa will need you later today, and I'll stay with your father then so he isn't alone."

Penny's face relaxed. A slight smile formed on her lips. "That's very thoughtful of you," she said, before slouching down in one of the chairs, and pulling her cell phone out of the pocket of her jacket.

Back at the house, Emily fed Jasmine and cleaned up the kitchen. She found the dirty scarf where she'd left it. *What should I do with it?* It wasn't something she could talk to Gus about at the moment. *Was this Annabelle's scarf?* There wouldn't have been anyone else near that garden, and certainly not Penny. Would Gus have kept any of Annabelle's things?

She decided to go up and check. All the closets were empty, except for Gus's closet in the master bedroom. *How can that be?* She had been years getting rid of Mark's things. She had worn several of Mark's flannel shirts just to feel close to him. But maybe it wasn't the same for men. In fact, she'd heard somewhere that if a man had been in a happy marriage before his wife died, he often married quickly.

And Gus had told her that he and Annabelle had been very happy. Anyway, she intended to put the scarf away for now as she didn't want Gus upset when he got home. As much as it had seemed strange to find a scarf in the dirt, it really didn't matter. It was almost certainly Annabelle's scarf.

Gus stared at the flashing lights on the monitor, felt the irritation of the plastic tube in his nose.

Stupid...stupid...stupid. Louise Sanderson from the shelter had been wearing that scarf when he'd killed her. He'd given it to her, to prove his love for her. She'd fought him when he forced the knife between her ribs. The rush he'd felt with the blood that spilled that night... He'd gone back to the house for a shovel, his mind operating at fever pitch. How had he missed the damned scarf? He closed his eyes, willing his mind back under control.

When Emily got to the hospital that evening, the staff at first seemed unwilling to let her into the room, citing a comment made by Penny about who could see her father. Emily explained that she was his fiancée and was here to see him, that she'd been the one who called the ambulance.

When they allowed her into his cubicle Gus seemed to be sleeping. She was told she could stay for fifteen minutes, and went to the waiting room to wait until she could go in again. She'd brought her iPad with her to check her emails using the hospital WiFi. When she finished she decided to search for Gus on the Internet. She'd never thought to do it before because he'd been very open about his life and his interests.

Yet, she owed it to Grace to check for what she could find. She wanted to prove to Grace that Gus was who he said he was. She didn't doubt it, but her daughter did, and that was reason enough to check.

Gus Parsons should be an easy search since he'd lived in Ontario for years. After a few minutes, she found two old addresses for him, one in Kingston and one in Barrie. There were several pictures of him working for service organizations in those two cities, but no mention of his personal life. But then again, not everyone was on Facebook or Instagram, especially being a man in his sixties with a busy life, and a daughter as difficult to deal with as Penny.

She didn't find anything earlier than five years ago, but she did find mention of an Angus Parsons who'd disappeared from a psychiatric hospital in British Columbia. He was found frozen to death months after he disappeared almost twelve years before.

Her search was interrupted by the nurse telling her that Gus wanted to see her. When she entered the room, he smiled and reached for her.

"I've been worried about you," she said.

"And I'm glad you're here. Penny told me you went home to look after Jasmine, that you and she are taking turns being with me. That's good. You have no idea how much better I feel now that you're here. Sorry I was asleep when you came in earlier."

"That's all right." She took his hand, felt the slight tremble in his fingers. "Are you worried about something?" she asked. "If you are, don't be. I'll look after everything at the house."

Have to stop her from going downstairs, somehow. Why not pretend the office is set up with an alarm?

"I don't think I told you, but I have security alarms on my office. I usually set the alarm and close the door, but with Penny so upset... I need you to simply close the door without stepping into the room. Can't always be sure that Jasmine won't take a stroll down there and set the alarm off. It's wired straight to the police station in St. John's, and you don't need a false alarm in the middle of all this."

Gus didn't look like himself... He seemed somehow tentative. *Is there something more going on with him? Is he hiding something about his health?* "Of course, I'll look after it."

"Thanks. Now, sit down and tell me how you're doing."

She slid into the chair next to his bed, doing a quick check of the intravenous and monitoring equipment. "I'm doing okay. I'm more worried about Penny. She was really upset when I called her about you going in an ambulance. She started blaming me, said I was trying to hurt you," she said, feeling her throat tighten. "Gus, it's difficult for me where Penny is concerned. I hate to mention it with you lying here in bed and worried about your health, but does she not realize that you and I are getting married? She acted as if I had no right to be here with you. Why would that be?"

I fucking do not need this shit!

"I'll talk to her. But in the meantime, I'm hoping to be out of here in a day or so. And when I do we will get going with our plans. This whole thing has shown me how easily life can change." He smiled slightly and grasped her hand.

"I'm sorry to be talking about these things when you're in here."

"No. I need to know when something is upsetting you. You're going to be my wife. We have to share whatever is going on with each other. Don't give it another thought."

"You're sweet." She stroked his hand where it rested on the sheet. "And we'll work out our plans. I assume you'll have an exercise program and nutritional counseling. I've already found a nutritionist in St. John's. She's agreed to come to the house when you get home."

"Maybe we should let the doctor decide."

"Medical doctors are not taught about nutrition. They will suggest you go on a low fat, low cholesterol diet with no follow-up. That's not good enough as far as I'm concerned."

"Nurse Carling to the rescue, is that it?" he asked, smiling at her.

"Yes. You're going to get out of here, get home and get

healthy. You're going to start taking time out of your day for a good walk, and you're going to eat healthy food."

"I'm going to do whatever you tell me to do. We're in this together, aren't we?"

She was reminded of Mark and how difficult he'd been about making changes after his first heart attack, how she'd worried. "I'm relieved to hear you say that."

CHAPTER TWELVE

W hen Gus was released from hospital the next day, Emily was waiting for him. When she saw him being wheeled toward her at the main entrance her heart pounded with relief. "No heart damage, just angina. A warning as Dr. Leigh said. He's wonderful, isn't he?"

"He sure is," Gus said, taking her arm as he stood up, giving the nursing aide a smile. "To think I still had to ride in one of those things, but it was a nice ride. Thank you," he said, stepping away. "But right now, all I want is out of here. I suppose you've got a healthy lunch planned for me." He squeezed her arm as he smiled down at her.

"More than that. We're going to start a walking regime as of tomorrow. You have today off, buddy, but after that, look out," she said, as she walked beside him out through the main door of the hospital into the bright sunshine. "And, by the way, I'm driving."

"Whatever you say, nurse," he said as they reached the car.

"That's the attitude," she said, as she got behind the wheel. They drove home without saying a word to each other. Gus seemed preoccupied, but maybe he was more worried about his health than he appeared. As they pulled into the driveway leading to the house, Gus tapped the dash, an impatient tap.

She glanced over at him, seeing the determined set of his jaw. Something was bothering him, and he had chosen not to share it with her. "We're almost there."

"Just anxious to be home."

There better not be anything out of place in my office.

"I don't want you going to your office today, please. You spend far too much time on all your work for the shelter and your business stuff. Let's take the afternoon off, watch a movie and relax."

Stop bossing, bitch!

When they entered the house, Jasmine greeted them with a sharp bark. "I think she needs to go out," Emily said.

"Why don't you look after her? I'll stay on the sofa and wait for you to come back."

"Promise?"

"Scout's honor." *I only need ten seconds to check to see if any camera shows any activity at all.*

Emily snapped the leash on Jasmine, anxious to take her out and then get back to Gus. She'd arranged for the nutritionist to visit that afternoon, knowing that like most people Gus would be more willing to listen to any dietary changes while his hospital visit was still clear in his mind. Sure, it was a bit of manipulation, but she had no intention of Gus not watching his diet and following an exercise program. History was not going to repeat itself, if she could help it.

Out in the clean, crisp air, Emily made her way down the driveway, studiously avoiding the entrance to the secret garden. The place no longer appealed to her. Last night she had lain awake trying to decide if she should talk to Gus about the scarf and decided that if he didn't bring it up, she wouldn't either.

After a lunch of carrot soup and kale salad, Emily and

Gus listened to the nutritionist talk about the foods he should concentrate on and the ones to avoid. She'd heard it all before, but Shelley Wilson had a very pleasant way about her.

"I think that's about all I have for you today," Shelley said.

"That's good because I really need to get down to my office for a few minutes," Gus said, looking from one woman to the other.

"Not for long," Emily cautioned.

When he left, Emily followed Shelley into the hallway leading to the front door. "He's a nice man. Have you lived here long?"

"I'm here visiting. We're planning to be married sometime soon. He has a daughter, Penny Parsons and a granddaughter Tessa who live in St. John's."

"Is that her?" Shelley asked, pointing to a framed photo on the wall.

"Yes."

Shelley looked closer, a small frown forming on her face. "I think I know her. She lived in my apartment building in Kingston a couple of years back. We got to know each other quite well. She invited me to her apartment, got to meet some of her friends... I'm sure she told me her father died in a boating accident."

"Can't be the same Penny Parsons. Her dad's alive and well, as you can see."

Shelley shook her head, a frown flickering on her forehead. "Weird. She looks just like the Penny Parsons I knew in Kingston," she said again.

"Or simply a coincidence. I'm sure that's what it is."

"You're probably right," Shelley said, picking up her jacket off the bench. She turned to Emily. "If you need any more information than what I've provided, or you need to speak with me, here's my card. Call me anytime."

"Thank you." Emily watched Shelley get into her car, her mind turning over what the nutritionist had said.

She returned to the kitchen, just as her cell phone started to ring. "It's working! I'll have to tell Gus so he won't worry," she said, picking it up. "Hi Grace, how's your day going?"

"Good. Did you get Gus home from the hospital okay?"

"Yes. He was glad to get out of there. His biggest complaint was the food."

"What did the doctor say?"

"Angina, but mild. Put him on blood pressure pills and told him to rest. He's down in his office right now. Gives a whole new meaning to the word *rest*."

"And you?"

"I'm doing fine. The nutritionist just left."

"Mom, I know what you're thinking, but this isn't like Dad. Angina is not a heart attack, only a warning as you know. I'm sure Gus will listen to you. After all, he's got his very own private nurse," she said in a teasing tone.

"But it still feels a little as if life is repeating itself."

"Don't think like that. Gus is not Dad. Dad wouldn't listen to you."

"Your father simply couldn't come to grips with the idea that he was not the man he once was. That's all."

"I know, Mom. And you are not responsible for what Dad refused to do. I want you to know that."

"I do, but the memories—"

"What was the nutritionist like?"

"Sweet. Very competent. And something really odd happened as she was leaving. She spotted a picture of Penny on the wall, and was convinced they had lived in the same apartment building in Kingston years ago. Can you believe that?"

"Did Penny live in Kingston?"

"I'm not sure."

"Well, you can always ask Gus about it. He'd know."

"You're right. Besides, the Penny Parsons she knew had lost her father in a boating accident."

There was a short pause before Grace spoke. "Mom, don't worry about it. We've all had moments when we think we recognize someone when we don't."

"She seemed so sure, though. But that's life. We all make mistakes."

"What's the nutritionist's name?" Grace asked.

"Shelley Wilson. She works for Dynamic Lifestyle in St. John's. I found her on the Internet. Aren't you proud of me? You're always saying I should be using my phone to do any searches I need."

"I am proud of you Mom. But I'm going to be late for a meeting. Talk to you tomorrow. Call me if anything changes, promise?"

"Sure. Have a good day, dear."

The next call came from the storage people in St. John's. They wanted her to meet them at the storage unit she'd arranged, as the items she'd had shipped from Boston had arrived.

She agreed to do that, but first she needed to get Gus to come up from his office and take a break. She hurried down the stairs and along the corridor to his office, stopping at the door. She expected to find the door closed, but instead she heard Gus talking in a very agitated tone to someone who was clearly putting him on the spot about something.

She couldn't let that happen. He was supposed to avoid stress. She strode into the room. "Gus!" she whispered, "who are you talking to?"

Jesus! First Penny. Now you.

He grimaced as he hung up. "Just a client who won't take no for an answer."

"Gus, darling, this is the kind of stress Dr. Leigh wants you to avoid."

"Didn't expect that particular call," he said, going to her and putting his arms around her. "It won't happen again."

This will all be over soon.

"You have to be careful, Gus. This attack was a warning."

"I know. It's just hard to suddenly call a halt to my life," he said, kissing her tenderly.

"I understand. I came down to tell you that the pieces I had shipped from home arrived. The storage people need me at the facility to sign them in."

His expression was quizzical. "Oh, you mean the things you had shipped over here from your house?"

"Yeah. Since our plans are still a little indefinite, I thought that I'd keep them in storage until we decide what we want to do with them."

He rested his hands gently on her shoulders. "Does that mean you'd be willing to move here? To sell your house in Boston?"

"I'm thinking about it."

Nice touch. Moving things. Marriage plans. Such a tidy bundle.

He took her hand. "Come on upstairs. I have something else for you to think about."

When they got to the living room, he pulled her down on the sofa beside him. "Emily, while I was in the hospital and had time to realize what was going on, what it could mean to us, I realized that I don't want to go any longer without marrying you."

"But—"

"I know we were going to work out a plan, take our time. But what if I don't have much time left? I don't mean to scare you."

Memories of the last hours with Mark filled her with remorse. Tears blurred her vision.

"Gus, I don't know if we should be talking like that. The doctor said all you needed was to take care of yourself, rest and relax. You'll be fine."

"I didn't mean it that way. I'm sure I'll be fine. It's just that when I was lying in that awful hospital bed, I realized that the single most important thing to me is you. You're all I want in this world.

"We have lots in common. We enjoy each other's company. We know we'll marry sooner or later. I want to make it sooner. I want us to settle in here and for you to make any changes you want in the house. We can even keep your house in Boston, if you'd like. Money's not an issue. Or you could rent it out to someone."

"Well, there was someone already inquiring about renting it."

"There. You see? It's fate. We're meant to be together. We can spend part of the year here. Part of the year in Boston and at my house in the Bahamas – or wherever we like. It's up to us. And right now, it's up to you. What do you say?"

"I...I don't know what to say. I need to get to the storage unit. They're waiting for me. Can we finish this when I get back?" she asked, smiling with happiness.

"It's a deal. I'll put champagne on ice. I'll call and have the hotel downtown prepare Shrimp Pernod and you can pick it up on your way home. I'll order extra broccoli just to please nutritionist Shelley. They always package it in insulated bags, and even if it's only warm, we can heat it up. That way, we don't have to cook on my first night home."

She kissed him quickly. "You never cease to amaze me."

"Why?"

"I'm still thinking about getting married and you've got dinner all planned."

"But I have the advantage. I've been thinking about this since I left here in an ambulance."

She laughed as she hugged him close, feeling his solidness, drawing in his strength. Ever since the first time they'd talked on FaceTime, she knew they shared so much, that they had a bright future ahead of them. She couldn't tell anyone that because they'd think she was just a naïve and needy older woman. But there had been something about him from the start. Something she found irresistible. "I'll be back as soon as I can."

As she drove into St. John's her mind was on Gus and what their life would be like as a married couple. Sure, there was the issue of Penny, but if they were going to travel, stay part of the year in Boston, and weeks in the Bahamas, Penny wouldn't be able to cause much upset in their lives. Besides, with a little effort she could probably convince him to leave St. John's for most of the year, given the fog and the isolation of living on a very large island away from everything.

She met with the moving company and the storage people to arrange for the unloading of her things. It was wonderful to see the restored desk she'd purchased years ago – one she really enjoyed. And the lamps and the antique blanket box that would provide her storage for off season clothes, and of course the loving old sewing machine her mother had given her years ago. It still worked, and she loved to use it.

When she reached the lobby of the hotel, they called the kitchen and a very bright red insulated box was placed in her car. Gus had looked after everything.

She was driving home, singing along to the radio when her phone rang. Clicking on the icon, she heard the voice of the managing partner in her husband's business, Alex Martin.

"I'm glad to hear from you, Alex. How's everything at Lexica?"

"Really great. I still wish Mark was here running the business with me. But you've been wonderful to work with since his passing. I thought I'd let you know we're going to call a board meeting for next month. I know you're away right now, but I wondered if you could give me some idea of when you'd be available so we can book an off-site boardroom and make dinner arrangements. We have a lot to celebrate. Business has been really good."

"Certainly. I'll need a little time to check my schedule. Can I call you tomorrow?"

"That would be great. Sylvia and I are planning to leave for California this weekend for a few days to see our daughter. She's gotten another promotion."

"Tell her I said hi, and congratulations, will you?"

"I will. Oh. Before I forget. There was a private investigator here asking questions about you the other day. Really odd. He talked to my assistant. She got his business card. A company out of Washington. When she tried to find out what he was after, he said he only wanted to know if you worked here. But Ellen thought he was being too nosy as he spent most of his time asking her about our company and what role you had in the business. He didn't get any financial information of value visiting the office, which made me wonder what he was really up to. Maybe it was another company doing a little leg work in preparation for offering to buy the company. What do you think?"

"I have no idea."

She just got off the phone when Grace called. "Mom, I need to ask you something."

"Sure. What dear?"

"It means I have to tell you something, but before I do I need to explain."

"I'm on the road. I'll pull over." She eased the car into a vacant lot and put it in park.

"You're probably not going to be pleased with me, but I've

been worried about your life in St. John's. Your phone issues, Penny's behavior. The fact that Gus is wanting to get married so soon. I need to tell you what I found out."

"Grace, is this necessary?"

"I think it is. Have you asked Gus why your phone wasn't working? Or did you just accept what he said?"

"I didn't have to ask him. He gave me a new phone within a day of me getting here. And I was able to talk to you in the house, so the problem's solved."

"Mom, why did Gus give you a new phone?"

"He said he wanted me to have the latest iPhone because he does. What's your problem?"

"Mom, there's something else. I can't find any record of Gus Parsons prior to him living in Ontario. And when you told me about Shelley Wilson thinking she knew Penny, I checked into that. Penny Parsons lived in the same apartment building as Shelley."

"How do you know it was the same one?"

"Our investigator has connections in Barrie and he says the building hasn't changed hands in years, that the owner is also the manager and he remembers both women living there. He specifically remembers Penny's red hair and her fiery temper. And it seems he had a bit of a thing for Shelley."

"You put your investigator on Gus? And you sent him to the Lexica offices as well?" Emily said, anger writhing in her stomach. "What are you trying to do?"

"Mom, no one went near Lexica. I can guarantee that. And if Penny said her father died in a car accident, what's going on?"

"Shelley could have made a mistake. We all make mistakes. But I'll ask her when she comes back for her follow-up visit with Gus."

"Speaking of Gus, why can't we find more out about him? If that's his daughter, he should be somewhere in the system.

People have all kinds of information on the web, yet Gus doesn't seem to have much and all of it is in Ontario and spans a very few years."

"So, what's wrong with that?"

"It's weird. As our investigator said, it's very unusual not to find birth records, work records, something. But for a couple of photos taken while he owned a company in Ontario, there's nothing."

"Grace, I'm really disappointed in you. The fact that you can't track his life further back than a few years ago, doesn't mean much of anything. He may have had reason to keep his whereabouts private. He is very knowledgeable about cyber security, and maybe he simply kept his information inaccessible. I would if I could." A thought struck her. "Maybe he worked for government security and led a life hidden behind some sort of security network. I don't know..."

"Mom, that's not likely. My big thing is I'm worried about you, about what's going on over there."

"Well, you're here next weekend for a visit, aren't you? We'll settle all your doubts when you come to visit."

"That's going to be a problem. I just got word that a trial I've been preparing for has been moved up. I have to be here next weekend to prepare."

Emily felt the tension ease in her body. Was she really worried about Grace being with them next weekend, given her attitude? Maybe this delay was a good thing... "Then, we will see you the weekend after that. In the meantime, Grace, please don't worry about me. We are doing well. In fact, I was just at my storage unit. The things I sent over are here and safe. I picked up dinner for Gus and me, and we're planning a quiet evening."

"Okay, Mom, and I'm sorry I can't come next weekend, but I promise I'll be there the following weekend."

"Come hell or high water?" Emily teased, remembering

that this had been one of Grace's and her father's favorite sayings.

"Come hell or high water," Grace said. "And I love you."

"Love you too."

Once on the highway she thought about what Grace had said. She'd discovered the same thing – a scarcity of information on Gus – when she went online while waiting in the hospital. But she hadn't shared that with Grace. There were certainly questions she needed answers to, but Gus had answered all her other questions. She had been concerned about the camera, but he had explained that. He would likely explain this as well.

When she drove up the driveway, Gus was waiting outside for her. When she got out of the car, he put his arms around her, hugging her close.

"I missed you. I know you were only gone a couple of hours, but it felt like a couple of weeks. That's the other thing that's happening to me. Whenever you're away from me, I miss you more than I ever expected. You've got to marry me," he said, kissing her, his lips urgent on hers.

The red insulated box with the food she was carrying nearly slipped from her hands as he pulled her close.

"Oh, God! What would I do if something ever happened to you?" he said, his words stressed and urgent.

"Nothing is going to happen to me, but our dinner might get cold if we stay out here much longer."

"Are you really hungry?" he asked, a strange look in his eyes.

"A little."

"Okay. I just need a few minutes to tell you a bit of news that I know you'll be as excited about as I am." He took the insulated box from her and she followed him into the house.

He put the box on the table before grabbing her hand and leading her into the living room and sitting down beside her on the sofa. "I called Jerry Green, the pastor. You remember him?"

"Yes."

"I told him we were getting married. He's thrilled. He says he'll do a service for us whenever we want it. And I want it as soon as possible. He's almost as thrilled as I am."

CHAPTER THIRTEEN

"So soon?" Emily asked, his words taking her breath away. "I don't know if this is a good idea. I mean, Grace can't come here until the weekend after next. She called while I was out and one of her trials have been moved up, now starting the Monday after she was supposed to be here with us. I want you to meet her before we get married."

Fucking fantastic! By the time the bitch gets here it will all be over.

"And we will. Why don't we choose a month from that weekend? We could visit with Grace, maybe plan that all of us go on a trip to the house in Bahamas for a family gathering. Sort a family wedding reception in the sun. What do you say?"

"Gus, I... I need to ask you something. I've never asked you about this before because it never came up."

Listened into the call. Got the answer ready.

"Ask me anything. We have no secrets from each other."

Emily shifted on the sofa, trying to find the words to ask about Gus's past, about what Grace had told her. "I... This is difficult."

STELLA MACLEAN

"Don't you worry about it. Simply ask me, whatever it is."

"Where did you live before you were in Ontario? I mean, ah, did you grow up in Ontario?"

"You want to know why there is no record of me before Ontario." He rubbed his hands together and took a deep breath. "I was involved in cyber security in Afghanistan and the Middle East. I can't tell you anything about it. I shouldn't be telling you that much, but you're going to be my wife and you need to know about it. I'm out of it now, and thankfully, still alive. But please don't ask me anymore about it as I cannot tell you. And most of all you cannot tell another soul. Not even Grace. If she asks again, tell her I grew up in British Columbia."

She took a deep breath, let it out slowly as she felt the strain lift from her heart and mind. "I knew there would be a good explanation. And I won't tell anyone anything."

You gullible, naïve woman-child. Little do you know that before the week is out you will be dead. And I shall miss your concern... but your money will make up for all of it.

"I know you won't my darling. And I'm am delighted to have you in my life. Let's have dinner. I've chosen a Spanish red from Rioja I'm sure you'll like. Then we can spend the evening listening to music and talking about the future." He took her hands in his.

Two hours later as they settled on the sofa, Gus pulled a notepad and pen from the drawer of the table. "I need to go over something with you." He turned to her, his eyes warm and caring, his smile making her heart lift in her chest.

She couldn't imagine being any happier than she was at this moment. All the earlier doubts, and the worry seemed to have fled. "Knowing you, you've thought it all out carefully," she said, wanting to snuggle in his arms rather than talk about anything serious.

"I have. I want everything to be taken care of, for us to be able to concentrate on our future together. We have children to consider, and they need to know that our affairs are in order. I admire Grace for being cautious where you're concerned. After all, she is your daughter and she wants the best for you."

"She does," Emily said, relieved that he understood.

"If we're going to be married in the next few weeks, we will need a marriage contract and new wills. But before we start talking about it, I need to tell you how I see it." He clasped her fingers tightly in his hand. "I love you and I want you to be my wife as soon as it can be arranged, but in the meantime, we need to sort things out."

"Okay," she said, wondering what was coming next.

"Emily, I've never loved anyone like I love you. You mean everything to me. You're kind, thoughtful and loving. I am going to put your name on all my assets and my companies. I want you to have everything, should I die."

"Oh. No! That's not right. We haven't been together very long." She pulled her hands from his. "What about Penny? And Tessa?"

"We've talked about this before. They've already been provided for in Penny's mother's will. Because of her mother's will, Penny is wealthy in her own right."

"But that doesn't mean she won't be hurt when she learns that you've left your estate to me. Gus, you need to think about this. You must leave her something. I don't need your money. You don't need mine. Why create a problem with your daughter?"

"I've already talked it over with her. She's the one who encouraged me to do what I want to do. Penny has more money than she'll ever need."

"But Gus, surely you'd like to leave money to the woman's shelter?"

"Yes, of course. But the bulk of my estate will go to you."

Now, my dear little dummy is the time for you to say what I know you will.

"Gus, my daughter is on the board of Lexica and holds her father's shares as an investment, along with money she inherited as well. Our children are very lucky, aren't they?"

"They certainly are," he said, his eyes on her.

She loved the feeling of being the center of his attention. "And the rest of my estate will go to you," she said.

"You don't need to do that," he said, a sigh escaping his lips.

"But I do, Gus. You're doing it for me. We're in this together. It's only reasonable that I do it for you. And I'll include the woman's shelter in my will. That way, if one of us passes, we'll be able to do something for the shelter. With our combined money, the possibilities are endless. What do you think?" she asked.

"That's a wonderful idea. I hadn't thought of it before, but whoever is left behind can create something lasting, in memory of our love and devotion to each other," he said, his smile warm and caring.

Emily worked her fingers into his shirt front as she snuggled closer. "There are so many good things we can do with our money. We can even start planning how we allocate the money now, if we want to."

She leaned away from him, looking up into his face, seeing the kindness in his eyes. "We could even turn this property into an animal refuge, not just dogs, but for other animals at risk."

"That's a great idea. So, you're all right with me getting a draft of these documents drawn up for us to review?" he asked, pulling her into his arms, his scent surrounding her, comforting her.

"By all means. We have a lot of planning to do in the coming weeks, so let's get these done."

"As long as you're okay with all of it. I'm not trying to rush you, but we need to get organized." He hugged her, his smile wrapping around her heart. "I can't wait to be able to call you Emily Parsons. We've got the whole world waiting for us, darling."

She looked into his eyes, and knew without a shadow of a doubt that Grace's worries about Gus and his intentions were groundless.

CHAPTER FOURTEEN

The next morning, after a sleepless night, Emily got up and took Jasmine out for a walk. Maybe she'd feel better with a good brisk walk. She didn't know what kept her awake last night, although there was something bothering her. Even though they'd made love last night, Gus went back to his room as he had done since she arrived.

She realized that they'd had a lot to adjust to; her learning about living in St. John's and him having to make accommodations for her being in the home he'd shared with Annabelle. She understood all that, but it didn't feel right that every night since she'd been there, she'd woken up alone. Lately, she'd been hoping he'd crawl in with her in the early morning, but that hadn't happened. Was she making too much of it? Was it simply a matter of time before they'd be comfortable sleeping the night together?

With Jasmine safely on her leash and the coffee starting to perk, she pulled on her jacket and headed out the back door into the early light. It was so crisp and cool out. The scent of pine trees filled her nostrils. What a beautiful spot. Jasmine raced ahead of her. "This morning, we're going to the secret garden," she murmured to herself.

Jasmine yipped and twisted her leash as she hurried ahead, forcing Emily to run behind her. "Slow up, Jasmine. You're breaking the driveway speed limit," she said, chuckling as she tried to keep up. She had come to love Jasmine. Part of it was missing her own dog, and part of it was Jasmine's sweet personality.

Once on the bench in the garden she settled in, her gaze taking in the deep shades of green, the mosses blanketing the ground leading to the other part of the garden. She loved it in here, her favorite part of the property.

And suddenly she knew what was preying on her mind, what had kept her awake last night. She needed to talk to Grace. She needed to have her daughter there with her as she prepared to get married. She needed her daughter's support and love.

Sure, they hadn't parted on the best of terms at the airport. And the last phone call had been a little strained, but she knew Grace loved her, and she would give her life for her daughter. At such a special time as this, they needed to be together. They'd go shopping together for dresses, have lunch out at a local restaurant and simply enjoy being with each other, in the place where she and Gus would probably live and call home.

She dialed Grace's number. Her daughter's sleepy voice came on the line. "Oh! I forgot about the hour and a half time difference. I'm sorry, Grace. I'll call back later."

"No, Mom. I'm awake. I was just lying in bed and wishing I didn't have to go to work today. My trial is not proceeding as well as I'd hoped. My client hasn't been honest and we may lose because of it."

"That's awful. What can you do?"

"That's what I'm meeting about today. We got a postponement to give us time to figure out our position going forward. Anyway, enough about me. How are you doing?"

"I'm doing really good. Gus and I are making our plans, hoping to hold a wedding here and then all of us will go to his house in the Bahamas. We're getting our wills and marital contracts organized. Gus is going in to his lawyer's office today to have a draft made of each document."

She heard her daughter's sharp intake of breath. "Mom, whatever you do, don't sign anything until you have an appointment with your own lawyer in St. John's. And fax me a copy of all the documents when you get them."

"That's what Gus said. And he's leaving his entire estate to me, and before you ask, Penny has already been taken care of in her mother's estate. Grace, I know you've been worrying about me, about me being taken advantage of by Gus. And I can understand that, given that Gus and I seem to be moving forward so quickly with our plans. But we're not young. We love each other. We don't believe in just living together. We want to be married."

Grace sighed. "Okay, Mom. Get the documents ready. I'll find a lawyer in St. John's for you, and call you with the name. Do you want me to make an appointment for you?"

"No. I can do that once you've given me the name."

"It may take me a day or two to find someone. In the meantime, don't do anything that would jeopardize your position. I realize how much you want to be married. But it's my responsibility to make sure it's done right."

"Grace, please be happy for me."

"Are you happy, Mom?"

"Yes. Gus is very good to me. We love one another. We enjoy each other's company. We plan to travel, and I'm not giving up the house in Boston. We're going to live part of the year in the Bahamas, part here, and part in Boston. And probably travel to Europe as well."

"Mom, that sounds wonderful. And I'm sorry for not being as enthusiastic as I should be."

"I know. You worry about me. But you don't have to."

"Mom, I can't help but worry about you. You're my mom, and I don't have brothers and sisters to boss around. You're it," she said, her tone gentle and caring. "I love you, Mom, and I want you to be happy. And if Gus is the one who makes you happy, then I'm fine with it. Besides, a nice week's vacation in the Bahamas would be wonderful."

"Thanks, dear. And I'll wait to hear from you about the name of the lawyer you find for me."

CHAPTER FIFTEEN

E mily sighed, part out of boredom and part from exhaustion. The past week and a half had been incredibly busy getting things organized for the weekend and her daughter's arrival. Grace had found a lawyer for her in St. John's and she had an appointment with the woman the weekend after Grace's visit.

Grace managed to get her trial issues straightened away, and she was due in on Saturday afternoon, in just two days. They planned to go straight to the shops in St. John's to find dresses. Although she and Gus hadn't set the wedding date, it would probably be sometime next month at the earliest. Emily didn't want to set a date until Grace was here with her. She needed to share all of this with her daughter as she missed her. It wasn't so much the dress shopping she was looking forward to as the time they'd spend looking, having coffee and simply enjoying each other's company.

She missed Grace terribly, something she could barely admit to herself or anyone else, especially not Gus. He believed she was very happy here, and she was. But she missed being able to be with Grace whenever she wanted.

She was also bored because Gus was away. It seemed that the shelter was still in a horrible financial mess. Gus had offered them enough to meet their payroll, but as he said, that had to be fixed. He'd been in his office all morning on the phone, before heading out to meet with bankers. He had to pick up the director of the shelter and take her along on this meeting, as well as the signing officer. It all sounded urgent and time consuming.

Jasmine had spent the morning following her everywhere. She kind of liked that devotion and had taken to talking to the dog as if she were human. "That had better stop soon, hadn't it, Jasmine?"

The dog wagged her tail and licked her lips, a sign that she expected a treat. "Your treat this morning is we are going into the library. I know that Gus hasn't shown any interest in the room, and I know why. Annabelle passed away there and the memory is simply too much for the man. But I think it's time you and I went in to see what sort of books we might find. We could sit in a comfy chair and read while we wait for Gus to come back. What do you think?"

As if the dog understood, she ambled down the hall toward the door leading to the library. Once inside the room, the light, the soft yellow walls with blue, white and burgundy furniture, a love seat in the corner by the window, a wall of books facing the windows, formed the most beautiful space Emily had been in for a very long time.

It was bright, inviting and open to the outside. There was a breath-taking view of the gardens and the woods beyond. "This is perfect," she whispered as Jasmine leaped onto the love seat and snuggled down, her eyes following Emily's every move.

Unable to take it all in, feeling that she'd found the part of the house that would be her favorite space, she moved to the bookshelves, shelves that reached to the ceiling. There were all sorts of books, from fiction to non-fiction, some with Annabelle's name on them, clearly books she wrote before she became ill.

Where to start?

Her eyes moved to a shelf that had a copy of *Eat Pray Love*, a book on her list of books she'd like to read. She'd not had time to read it as yet, despite everyone recommending it to her. She had a table full of books to be read at home, all of which were waiting for her to decide their fate. For now though, she'd simply enjoy her reading time there.

She reached for the book, and inadvertently knocked a small notebook that had been propped on the shelf, onto the floor. She reached down, picked it up and a piece of paper slipped to the floor. She gathered it up and was about to put it back in the book when she spotted someone's handwriting on the open page.

She didn't want to snoop, but she was curious to know something about the woman who had meant so much to Gus. She held the book, reading the lines the woman had written. Words about how kind Gus was being while she was ill, how much she appreciated everything he did for her despite the fact that he had work of his own to do.

The writer made notes of things that had gone on in their life, his long hours at the shelter, and how she missed him. Emily could easily relate to Annabelle and her sentiments. There were notes on books Annabelle had read, and personal comments about people she had conversations with. Guiltily she put the notebook back on the shelf.

As she reached to return it to its position on the shelf, she spied another camera, the same small black box, but no little red light on it. Gus must have forgotten to take this one away too – like the one in the living room. She put things back, and picked up the book she planned to read, tucking herself into a plush blue velvet armchair in the opposite corner.

But she couldn't seem to concentrate. The camera remained stuck in her thoughts. The day Gus had shown her the computer with the video feeds of all the cameras on the outside of the house, she'd listened carefully. And afterwards, she'd taken the time to make notes when she went upstairs. Notes on how to run the video and which of the computers to use. It all seemed strange to her – and so natural to Gus. She envied him that, his ease with technology, while the things she didn't know stuck out like the proverbial sore thumb.

And she wanted to show him that she could learn to use the technology in their home, not just her iPad. She'd worked hard to master all functions of her new cellphone, even though parts of it had seemed useless to her. Jasmine got up and came over, placing her soft head on Emily's leg. She patted the dog as an idea formed in her head.

Maybe she could go down to his office and check out the cameras showing the outside of the house. She was pretty sure she had her notes in the kitchen drawer, and she wanted to see if she could do it. Surely Gus wouldn't mind. She'd tell him when he got home about what she'd done. Besides, she wanted to see if she could run the cameras.

"What do you think, Jasmine? Should we go down and see what we can do?"

The dog's ears perked up.

"I knew you'd be game," she said, putting the book aside.

Emily switched on the lights at the top of the stairs, and Jasmine loped down ahead of her. When they reached the bottom of the stairs, a pale shaft of light shone through the crack of the office door. Had Gus left lights on? Jasmine moved slowly, sniffing the floor, making her way along the hall to the office.

Oh! What if the alarm was on in there? Hadn't Gus said that if anyone tripped the alarm, it would ring at the police station? That idea was too embarrassing for words. "Jasmine! Wait for me," she rushed ahead, hoping to grab the dog's collar. Too late. Jasmine nosed the door open and ambled into the room...

Emily waited, fearing the worst. She waited. Nothing. Not a sound.

"I guess it's okay," she said, following Jasmine into the room.

Once inside she noted that two of the four computer screens were on. One showed the stock market charts. The other showed the camera displaying the patio facing the tennis courts. She watched, waiting to see if any movement would trigger the camera to adjust. Nothing happened. It all seemed ordinary...boring actually. Digging her notes out of her pocket, she checked her instructions. A few clicks of the keyboard, and she went to other outside cameras. It was amazing how clear the images were. She found the camera that pointed down the driveway and one that showed the secret garden and the new bench. Toggling the joy stick she was able to get a really good closeup of the bench. "Wow," she said out loud.

Jasmine gave a sigh and lay down at her feet. Emboldened, Emily clicked on the file of cameras positioned inside the house. There shouldn't be any of them working. Yet, she had found one still in the library. *Don't start doubting Gus. Remember the business about his life before Ontario.*

The first camera listed was the kitchen. She hadn't noticed any camera in the kitchen. She clicked on it. Suddenly the kitchen appeared on the screen. No movement, completely still... She looked closer. Wasn't that her purse sitting on the counter where she left it this morning? That couldn't be... She leaned back in the chair, making it squeak, startling herself. *What's going on?* These cameras weren't supposed to be on. And she hadn't seen any in the kitchen.

She leaned in toward the screen, reading down the list. There was a library camera, the one she'd found. She clicked on it, and the room appeared...and the book she'd started to read was lying on the table next to the chair she'd sat in. A chill ran through her.

He said he'd removed all the cameras. But the one she'd found in the library had no red light showing. She believed him when he said they didn't work without the light, but clearly they did. Or there was more than one in the room. She checked her notes to see how to scroll back. Gus said the cameras only recorded when there was movement in the space.

Maybe she'd get to see Annabelle in the library... Wasn't that a little sick? she thought to herself, but hit the key that would rewind the tape. She was watching, her mind still going over the fact that the cameras were on even without a visible red light. Suddenly there were people and flashes of color, swirls of white, arms flailing. She rewound the video.

CHAPTER SIXTEEN

As if in slow motion the video began to play a scene filled with indescribable horror. Her eyes wide with disbelief, Emily stared at the screen, at the sight of Gus holding a woman down on some sort of bed, and Penny shoving a pillow in her face. The woman's hands scratched and tore, scratched and tore and finally, as if in slow motion the hands slid away. Penny continued to press on the woman's face.

Shock and terror tore through her mind, taking her breath as she grabbed the desk. Tears surged down Emily's cheeks. Her breath came in gasps, her screaming finally lowered to a whimper. "They... Oh God..."

She gasped, pushing the chair away from the desk as she struggled to stand. Her legs shook. Her head hurt; her mind seemed frozen by the image. "Turn away," she pleaded with herself. "Turn away..."

Gradually her legs took her weight. She was aware of Jasmine's soft moans as she steadied herself against the desk. She had to get upstairs, out of the house before Gus came home. He was a murderer... Her knees shook. She grabbed the edge of the filing cabinet to steady herself. She had to get out. Her purse with the car keys... Yes, it was on the kitchen counter. She steadied herself as she struggled to clear her mind of the images, the terror that drained her of any ability to think, to comprehend...

A door slammed somewhere.

Jasmine gave a soft whine as she headed out the door, disappearing toward the stairs.

Voices getting louder. Gus. Penny.

Oh, please God, Emily begged – her breath blocked, her mind frozen. They were coming along the corridor, arguing, Penny cursing. Gus swearing, a low guttural, dangerous sound.

"Where the hell is the bitch?" Penny demanded.

"Upstairs probably, reading one of her stupid books." Gus's voice filled her ears.

They were headed toward her, their voices growing louder.

Frantically she searched the room. *Where can I hide? What? Oh! God! No!*

Stumbling, fighting the trembling in her legs she got in behind the door of the office, her lungs burning from lack of air. She hardly dared swallow or breathe in case they heard her. Her mind searching frantically for what to do, she pressed into the tiny space, praying the door would hide her.

"For the last time," Penny screamed. "You're killing her tonight."

"Will you shut the fuck up? She might hear us."

"She'd better hear us. You're my husband and she's a dead woman. Because I know you slept with her, you stupid ass," Penny said. A shuffling sound, the squeal of a chair sliding along the floor smacking against the wall, then Penny's voice again. "Gus, someone's been at your computer."

"Christ!" Gus hissed.

A silence during which Emily held her breath, trying to focus.

"What is this?" Penny swore. "You were watching this without me? This is ours. Ours together," she yelled, a hard, smacking sound and something falling to the floor. Emily covered her mouth, blocking the sob, clawing at her throat.

"I wasn't watching anything. Stay here. I'm going upstairs to look for her. The Audi's still in the garage. The bitch must have been in here looking at these."

"Wait! How would she know how to work your precious system? You said she was really stupid when it came to tech stuff. She couldn't have done this... Oh...I get it. You played Mr. Smart Ass and showed her, didn't you? You were down here with her, bragging, showing her how to work your fancy system."

A wild scream, then a body crashing into the door, that in turn slammed into Emily's nose. Blocking a scream, she crouched down, covering her nose with her bloodied hands. The sounds of a vicious struggle, someone smashing into metal, a grunt of pain. "Penny, I'm going to kill you."

"Not if I kill you first. *You ruined everything!*" she screamed. "Everything!"

Crouching low, she watched in horror as Gus grabbed Penny by the neck and threw her against the wall across from where she hid. *They'll see me if they turn!* Transfixed by what was unfolding in front of her, the violent punches he aimed at Penny's body, her grunt of pain, galvanized Emily.

She had to leave. She had to take a chance. Grabbing the lower part of the door frame, she eased forward.

Penny screamed and kicked Gus in the crotch. He grunted and grabbed her hair, pulling her to the floor with him. They rolled away from her, tearing at each other like wild animals.

Now!

She scrambled around the door, heedless of whether they saw her, focused solely on the corridor. She ran to the stairs, the sound of grunts and cursing filling her ears. She had only seconds if they'd seen her. Minutes if they didn't. There was no way out of the house without setting off the chimes of a door opening.

Her lungs begging for air, she took the stairs two at a time, nearly falling at the top. Recovering quickly, she raced into the kitchen. Her fingers grasped her purse and she headed for the door. She hesitated for a split second. She needed a breath because the minute she opened the door Gus would know.

She pulled her keys out of her purse, her fingers trembling as she held the key fob for the car. Forcing air into her lungs, she listened to see if they were following her.

Not wasting another second, she went out the door to the car. She climbed in, started the car and tore down the driveway, skidding sideways as she accelerated. Once out on the road, she hit the gas pedal and the car leaped. Her hands shaking on the wheel, she tried to remember the route to the airport. She'd made a mistake at one of the turns a few weeks ago. "Pray to God, I don't do that again," she said, her voice sounding weak in her ears.

She needed to concentrate on the road. She glanced in the rearview mirror. Nothing behind her yet.

She drove faster, her tires squealing as she turned hard, the vehicle shuddering on the pavement. She couldn't let herself think about what just happened, couldn't trust herself to keep going if she did. The sight of the ocean lapping on one side of the highway and steep hills looming on the other side, sent waves of fear through her. Somewhere ahead there was an open stretch of highway; there had to be.

If Gus caught up with her, where could she hide? She drove away from the water, around a sharp curve onto a flat open area, a large green sign for St. John's a welcoming sight. She drove faster, her first moment of hope that she might make it to the airport rippled through her.

Taking a breath, blood gushed from her nose onto her upper lip. Ignoring the mess, she tapped the phone icon on the screen. Grace's number popped up. She hit the icon and waited for it to connect. "Hi Mom, how are you doing?"

"Grace, I need help," she said, sobbing in relief at her daughter's voice. "I'm in trouble. I've got to get out of here."

"Mom! Where are you?"

"I'm on the highway headed for the airport. It's horrible! It's all horrible," she gasped.

"What is?"

"Gus. Penny." Her body began to shake.

"I'm relieved you've finally come to your senses. Mom, listen to me," Grace said, her voice filled with worry, "I want you to leave there now, get to the airport, get your ticket and get through security just as fast as you can."

"He's killed other people."

"What!"

"I was in his office. He and Penny; they killed Annabelle! I saw the video," she cried, sobs shaking her body. "I'm afraid they're going to catch me before I can get to the airport."

"No! Mom. No. Just keep driving... I'm calling the police in St. John's right now. Please stay calm. We'll get you out of there. I promise. In the meantime, you pay attention to your driving, don't have an accident. I'll be back to you just as soon as I've contacted the police."

"Grace, I don't know if I can. I'm scared. He plans to kill me. He said it. He plans to kill me. I need help!"

"Mom. Please just focus on your driving. Get to the airport. I'll make sure the police find you. Call me once you're inside the building."

A dump truck roared down the highway toward her. She

pulled over a little and felt her rear tire catch on the edge of the pavement. "No!"

"Mom!"

The truck swerved out of the way. The heavy Audi settled back. "I'm okay. I'm going to drive as fast as I can. I'll call you once I'm inside."

She clicked the off button, jammed her foot into the gas pedal and steadied her hands on the wheel. "I will not let him catch me. No matter what it takes. I will not let him catch me." She said the words over and over.

The phone rang again. The screen showed "Gus Parsons." She couldn't answer it.

It kept ringing and ringing, the sound reverberating in her head. "I'll lie to him, let him think I've just gone for groceries...milk and butter...whatever." She clicked the button.

"Emily, where are you?"

"I'm going to the grocery store."

"You sound out of breath."

"No. I just had a scare. A truck nearly hit me."

"Where are you?"

What could she say? "I'm lost I think. I'm going to the store."

"Tell me the truth. You heard Penny and I arguing and it scared you, didn't it?"

She didn't answer. Ahead she could see an intersection. The airport couldn't be far now, could it?

"I'll be home soon," she lied, slowing down a little to read the signs.

"Okay. Enough. You're not going to the grocery store, unless you think there's one near the airport."

"What?"

"You're nearly to the airport." She heard a car door slam and the sound of an engine starting. "Wait right where you are," he ordered. "I'm coming for you."

She clutched the wheel, her mind whipping from one thought to another. *He knows where I am. How?* She stared at the phone on the seat next to her as she slowed down, trying to think.

What had the man at the electronics store said about Gus? He could track anything. Did that include phones and cars? Did he have something on the car or the phone to know where she was?

With one hand she rolled down the car window, the cold chilled air striking her cheek. Switching hands, she tossed the phone out the window into the oncoming traffic. Oh! What had she done? Now she couldn't call Grace. Tears spurted from her eyes. Fear made her body shake, her foot easing off the gas pedal, the car beginning to slow down.

Horns honked behind her.

Should she pull over?

No! She needed to keep going. She had to get to the turnoff to the airport. She accelerated, the tires squealing. Somewhere behind her she heard sirens. Glancing quickly in the rearview mirror, she saw a police car its lights flashing. She pulled over, her heart leaping in her chest. She couldn't be caught speeding. Gus would catch her for sure.

Maybe Grace had gotten through to the police in St. John's. Maybe the police car was coming to escort her to the airport. She eased to the side of the road. The police car eased in behind her. The officer got out and came toward her, his hand resting casually on his waist above his hip.

"Ma'am, Office Greg Neilson, Royal Newfoundland Constabulary." He pointed to her face. "You're bleeding. Are you okay?"

She pulled a tissue from her purse, as she tried to come up with an explanation. "Yes, I'm fine. I bumped my nose...

against the door frame." *Would he believe her? Would he tell Gus?*

"I didn't mean to scare you. I'm not going to give you a ticket. Is your name Emily Carling?"

"It is," she said, relief running through her, air escaping from her lungs. "Did my daughter Grace call you?"

"What? No. Gus Parsons called me, told me to be on the lookout for your vehicle. He said you were lost."

"No. I'm not lost. I need to get into St. John's to pick something up." She met the man's gaze, giving him what she hoped was a meaningful look. "I...I'm planning a surprise for Gus's birthday. I have to get to town to pick something up without him knowing about it. Then I got lost. I'm not that familiar with the roads. Only been here a few weeks. The roads are narrow. I gave myself a scare back there. Just need to get to town. It's a long way into town and back and I'm in a hurry," she said, spilling the words into the air.

The officer held up his hand. "That's okay. Really, Ma'am. Gus asked me to check on you. Your phone isn't working."

She glanced around, her mind searching for an explanation. "I dropped it. I didn't mean to. I dropped it," she repeated.

Again, he held up his hand. "That's fine. I'll call him back and tell him you're safe. Hope Gus appreciates what you're doing for him. He's a lucky man," the officer said, stepping back, offering her a friendly smile.

As she looked up into his kind face she considered telling him about Gus, about what she had witnessed. But she remembered Gus's story about Officer Neilson being a friend of his and Annabelle's. If he knew what she'd witnessed would he protect her from Gus? Not likely.

This young man would never believe that Gus was capable of such horrible things. Her body trembling, she forced a smile. "I'd better get going," she said, putting the car in drive.

"Drive safely," the officer said.

"I will," she said, easing back onto the highway. She could see the officer in the rearview mirror. He was on his cell phone. *Is he calling Gus?*

And if he was, Gus could be on the road now, not far behind her.

A few feet ahead, the highway turned, blocking the officer's view. As she moved into the turn she slammed the gas pedal to the floor and the car leaped, the engine roared. Every second counted.

Her eyes flicked to the rearview mirror. No sign of a police car. If Gus told the officer to catch her and stop her, she'd be finished. There was no way he'd believe that someone like Gus planned to kill her. Instead, she'd be labeled a crazy woman and she'd soon be back in Gus's clutches. Fear gripped her. The low hum of the car seemed more like a threat than protection as she sped along.

She forced herself to take a deep breath. If she could make it to the airport, get her ticket purchased, she'd be able to get through security. Once inside security she could find someone to help her.

Finally, a long straight stretch of road she recognized. She was pretty sure the road went to the left and into the airport zone.

She was driving so fast, she nearly missed the turn. The car skidded as she fought to make it onto the street. Her eyes scanning the rearview mirror again, she swung through the turn and toward the main entrance. She pulled the car into a space in the parking lot across from the door, grabbed her purse and raced toward the sliding doors.

Once inside, she hurried to the ticket agent, opening her purse searching for her return ticket as she approached the counter. It wasn't there. She put her purse on the counter, her fingers clawing through every part. "Where is it?" she muttered, clasping the purse, fearful that Gus had taken it.

Then, suddenly she remembered. She'd put it in the outside pocket of her purse. Relief making her hands shake, she yanked the paper out and passed it to the ticket agent. "I need to use this to get to Boston as soon as possible."

The agent gave her an assessing glance and Emily was glad she'd already wiped most of the blood off her face and hands. "Return?" the agent asked.

"No." She glanced over her shoulder. There didn't seem to be anyone watching her. She turned back to the agent. "Please hurry."

The agent's fingers clacked over the keyboard. "Ma'am, give me your credit card and once I confirm the original ticket was purchased using it, I can rewrite your ticket and get you through Montreal to Boston. You'll arrive in Boston at 11:45 Boston time. The flight leaves here in a little under three hours, connecting through Trudeau in Montreal. Is that okay?"

"Yes. Please hurry," she said, shoving her credit card across the counter.

The agent took the ticket from her, suspending it between her fingers. "Ma'am, are you sure you're all right?" She pointed at her face. "You've got some blood on your nose."

"Oh. I bumped into a door on my way here." She forced a smile as she retrieved another tissue from her purse and wiped her face again. Pain shot up her nose, bringing tears to her eyes. "I need to go through...now," she urged, her eyes sweeping the space behind her. *Where is Gus?*

After what seemed like hours, the agent gave her the boarding pass, and her credit card. "You're in row 1, seat A, the window seat. You can wait in the lounge until boarding. Have a good flight."

Emily ran to the stairs leading up to security and the gate area. A quick glance back showed no sign of Gus. But in glancing back, she tripped, landing hard on her knee. Yelping in pain, she hobbled up the remaining steps to the counter. Her knee burned. Her eyes watered with the pain. She had to make it through the document check-in area and into the security line.

Passing her boarding pass and passport to the security person, she waited while he checked it all over. He glanced at her several times, a frown on his face.

"I hit my nose on the way in here," she said, trying to explain the mess on her face. Can these people not go faster? she thought to herself, her eyes searching the stairs she'd just climbed.

"No luggage?" he asked, reviewing the ticket."

"Not this trip." The lie seemed to satisfy him.

"Thank you, ma'am," he said, pointing toward the lineup waiting to go through security. She moved to the end of the line, and as she did, she wondered if Gus knew someone here who might help him reach her in the line. She didn't know and she was worried.

Putting her weight on her right knee, eased the throbbing of her left one. When she looked up the line she saw four people ahead of her... Four women her age, one with a cane...all with carryon luggage and purses.

Please God...

She put her credit card away in her wallet, her fingers doing a shaky dance over the leather as she tried to force the recalcitrant card into its slot. She'd have to call Grace as soon as she got into the gate area. But she didn't have a cell phone... Her heart pounding, she watched as two more people moved to put their things on the conveyor belt, a woman reaching awkwardly around her cane to heft her carryon up on the conveyor.

Two more...

A sudden movement near the top of the stairs caught her attention. Gus stood there, his back to her, looking down the steps he'd just climbed.

Emily froze. *He bought a ticket.*

Frantic, she turned back, her mind feverishly searching for a way to get inside the gate and hide. She didn't dare look back. She would lose her nerve. She had to move. Now.

She glanced at the two women ahead of her. The woman at the front of the line had a soft smile on her face as she waited. The other woman was rooting in her purse, frowning.

Without thinking, she stepped ahead of her, leaned in close to the other woman and whispered. "Can I please go ahead of you. Please. There's a man coming behind us. He's after me. I'm afraid of him."

"Should we call the police?" the woman asked, her face wreathed in a worried frown.

"I'm going to call the police once I'm inside and safe. But if he catches me here before—"

"But where will you hide inside? We need to call the police, now."

"He has connections with the police. If he's able to stop me from going through security, I won't have a hope of getting away from him. Please, just let me go ahead of you," Emily pleaded close to tears. Her head pounded. Her heart thrummed in her chest. If Gus caught her now...

"By all means," the woman said, stepping back.

"Thank you," she breathed. "Thank you so much."

With her heart racing, Emily slipped ahead, placed her purse on the conveyer, her mind flooded with fear. Gus was only three people behind her. *Where can I hide inside? The bathroom? Can the gate staff help me?*

When she got to the officer, he looked at her ticket and her passport. "You're flying to Montreal, connecting to Boston. Are you traveling alone? And what happened to your face? Do you need medical care?"

"I don't need medical care. I hit my nose," she repeated the words, her frustration building. "I'm going to wash my face once I get inside."

"And you're traveling alone?" he asked again.

The woman in Montreal customs had asked her why she was traveling alone on her way to Newfoundland, before taking her aside to question her about where she was going and what she was doing. If security stopped her now... Remembering the frustrating time she'd spent with the agent in the customs hall in Montreal, she lied.

"I'm meeting someone inside. And I need to get to her. She's worried about me. I had to park the car. It took longer. Then I fell and hit my knee. Then it was hard getting up the stairs. And I need to help my friend." She knew she was babbling lies but couldn't stop herself.

"Go ahead," he said, begrudgingly, as if he'd hoped to find something wrong with her paperwork.

She gathered her things and walked as quickly as she dared, favoring her sore knee, toward the gates. Around the corner she saw the sign for the bathrooms.

Once inside, she hobbled into a cubicle and locked the door. Her throat tightened as she steadied herself against the wall. Fear made her knees weak. She sank down on the toilet seat, clutching her purse in her lap, her feet nervously tapping on the tiled floor. She struggled to take a deep breath.

Is there anyone else in here? Did anyone see me come in? And if so, would they tell Gus where I am?

She stood up quietly, easing further back in the cubicle, her breath loud in her ears. She couldn't hear anything. She listened with her whole mind. Nothing.

Am I safe? She couldn't be sure. She wished the toilet had a lid she could sit down on comfortably while she waited for her mind to clear. She had to figure out what to do, who to trust.

Yet, all she could think of was the raw rage she'd heard in Gus's voice those terrifying minutes in his office. He would find her no matter what it took, no matter what lies he had to tell. And if he convinced the check-in person that he was traveling with her, she feared they'd put him in the seat next to her. Her seat was a window seat which meant she'd be trapped if he got the aisle seat. He had a ticket and he would make sure she didn't make the Boston flight.

Take a deep breath... In... Out.

The sound of hurried footsteps on the tiles made her pulse spike. Someone went into the cubicle next to her. She moved as far into the opposite corner and leaned down. Black army boots?

Am I in the men's bathroom?

She'd gone into the wrong bathroom. But she hadn't seen any urinals.

She waited, barely able to breathe, her throat tight, terrified that the next person through the door would be Gus and she would be trapped.

The person coughed, flushed the toilet and left the cubicle. Water running and a cellphone ringing allowed Emily a second to siphon air into her lungs.

"Yeah," a voice said. *A woman's voice?*

She searched the cubicle looking for a crack wide enough for her to peek out. Nothing.

"I know, Mom, but I can't fucking deal with him right now." Clearly a female voice.

"You'd be swearing too if you had to put up with his whining about me seeing other people."

"Okay..." The click of disconnection reverberated around the cold walls.

Can I trust this person? Do I have a choice?

She stepped out of the cubicle, her wobbling knees getting her as far as the sink. She glanced in the mirror, saw the mess on her face and glanced at the young girl next to her. There was a scowl forming along a line of what looked like barbed wire between her eyes. Her lips were painted black.

"Could you help me?" Emily asked, her voice a croak.

"What happened to you?" the girl asked, turning to look at her. "Did somebody hit you?"

"Someone slammed a door into my face."

"Bummer," the girl said.

Emily couldn't help but notice the studded leather collar on the girl's neck, a tiny metal chain dangling from her jaw, a crucifix swaying gently at the end of the chain.

"I heard you on your cellphone. I...I lost mine on the way here. Could I borrow yours? I'll pay you for the call," she said, hastily.

"Are ya'll right?" she asked. "You look like hell."

Emily smiled for the first time in hours. "I feel like hell. I just escaped from a...a relationship. I need to call my daughter and tell her I'm okay."

"*You* calling *your* daughter? That's a new one on me."

"You have no idea," Emily said, pathetically grateful to be talking to this young woman who knew nothing about what she'd just been through. "I think I was followed in here by a man. He's a criminal."

"There's a lot of them around," the girl said, holding her phone out to Emily.

177

"I'll pay you, I promise," Emily said, reaching her hand out.

"Mom pays my cellphone bill. It's on her. It's the least she can do, after letting my shitty boyfriend know I'm on my way back to Montreal."

Tears of relief burned her eyes as Emily dialed Grace's number.

"Mom. I've been frantic. I've gotten through to the police in St. John's. It took forever. I'm still not sure they believed me."

"Oh Grace, you need to get back to them for me."

"Where are you?"

"I'm in the gate area, but I think Gus bought a ticket and followed me in here. I'm in the bathroom hiding." She glanced at the young girl, noting the scowl of concern. "I borrowed a phone. I had to toss mine out on the way here."

"*He's there?* Are you sure?"

"I saw him in line behind me. I don't know if he saw me. I convinced a woman to let me go ahead of her in the security lineup."

"Mom, you need to get to the gate and tell them you're in danger. I'm going to call... Just a minute I'm calling the St. John's police on the other line."

Emily waited, her eyes fixed on the girl's face. Her deep brown eyes were kind. Her smile warm and caring, something Emily desperately needed right now. She nodded slowly. The girl nodded back, gave her the thumbs up.

"Mom. Can I speak to the person with you?"

"Sure." She passed the phone to the girl. "My daughter Grace needs to speak with you."

"Me?" she asked, pointing at her chest, her eyebrows raised. The chain on her chin circled gently. She took the phone. "Yes?" she said.

"My name's Kat Summers."

Emily watched as the girl's expression went from quizzical to fearsome. "The bastard!" She stared at Emily. "Don't you worry. I'll look after your mom. And I'll find him," she said, her eyes focused on the wall behind Emily.

"What did Grace say?" Emily asked, watching the girl click off.

"You're to stay here. I'm going out to the gate to tell them what's going on. What does this man look like?"

Emily described him as best she could, her mind stuck on the idea that he might be waiting just outside the door of the bathroom. "Kat, please be careful. He's a very dangerous man. He can't find me. I'm afraid he'll find a way to get me away from here."

"No. He won't. I've been dealing with asshole men all my life. Trust me. There isn't anything they could try that I haven't seen before."

Grace gripped the edge of the counter for support. "Thank you, Kat."

The girl smiled. "You stay here. If someone comes in, slip into a cubicle and stand on the toilet. That way whoever comes in won't know you're here. Don't worry about them seeing you above the cubicle. Most people are too busy doing their thing to look up. You'll be safe until I get back." She opened her backpack and handed her a ball point pen.

"A pen?" Emily asked.

"If he figures out you're in here, and comes looking for you, you'll need this. Not much of a weapon, but if you jab him with it, you might surprise him, gain a few seconds to get away. And remember scream, scratch and run. Keep running until you reach the gate." Kat held out her arms.

Emily hugged her close, tears flooding her cheeks. "I...I... Hurry back."

"I will. Stay here!" With that the girl turned and strode out, her heavy boots making a smacking sound on the floor.

Emily glanced around, hugging her purse to her side, deciding finally that maybe the best thing to do was to hide in the cubicle and stand on the toilet if she had to. She clutched the pen tight in her fist, pressing her hand to her mouth to stop the sobs suddenly forcing their way into her throat.

Inside the cubicle, she waited but heard nothing except the sound a tap dripping and voices somewhere outside the cold, bare room. A public service announcement about not leaving luggage unattended. Somewhere a baby cried. She strained to hear any sound of Gus, fearful yet anxious to know where he might be.

Slowly the stress of the past hours began to seep through her, taking her courage with it. What would she do if Kat didn't come back? What if Gus came in there? The flight was not going for at least another couple of hours. How could she manage to stay hidden for so long? Gus was likely out there charming the gate attendants, asking if she'd checked with them.

And there were three people waiting ahead of him when she jumped the queue. Would one of them be willing to listen to his story? Listen and then come in here looking for her? Gus had to have figured out by now that she was hiding somewhere, and the bathroom was the obvious place.

How she wished she had a phone. She needed her daughter's calm, resolute voice.

Suddenly there was someone outside the cubicle, moving around. She waited, wondering, hoping...

She gripped the pen, her hand on the wall to steady herself.

CHAPTER SEVENTEEN

Emily heard someone moving along the cubicles, entering each, letting the door snap closed as they moved closer. She stepped back further into the cubicle. She clutched the pen tighter, her nails digging into the palm of her hand.

"Are you there?" a voice whispered.

Emily huddled closer to the wall.

"It's me. Kat."

"Oh!" Emily yanked open the door and nearly fell into the young woman's arms. "I thought you were him," she said, her voice shaking with relief.

"And I didn't know your name. I got out to the desk, went to tell the gate agent about you and didn't know your name or where you were going. The agent blew me off. Probably thought I was on something... *As if*." She shook her head, a wry expression on her face.

"I'm Emily Carling."

"A little late, but okay, I guess." Kat swiped a strand of black hair off her face. "I checked everyone waiting for the flight. Thankfully, there's only one flight going out in the

181

next two hours. I didn't see anyone that looked like the man you described. But I can go back out, give them your name and get them to send someone in."

"No. Let's go together. I can't bear being in here alone any longer"

"Then, you'd better clean the blood off your face," Kat said, pointing at her cheek.

"Again? Will this ever stop bleeding? They wouldn't believe a word I said looking like this, would they?"

"They'd probably wonder about a woman with wild eyes and blood on her cheeks," Kat said, a grin on her face.

Emily grabbed some paper towel out of the dispenser, ran water over it and cleaned her cheek and her nose. "There. Better?"

"Absolutely."

"Speaking of deranged women with wild eyes, I saw a truly deranged bitch."

Emily's heart skipped a beat, her breath stopped. "Did she have curly red hair?"

"Yeah. And swearing at the gate agent, yelling she needed to find her mom who had just come through security. One scary bitch, let me tell you."

Penny? "Kat. Do me a favor. Go back out and see what she's doing."

Kat's black lips formed a perfect 'O'. She blinked. "This is important, isn't it?"

"Just check for me. Don't let her see you coming back in here--"

"You bitch!" Penny growled, a guttural sound, her eyes wild as she stood at the entrance to the bathroom. "I'm going to kill you!"

"Run! Kat! Get help!" Emily stepped back. Her arm slammed into the paper towel dispenser sending pain ricocheting into her shoulder.

"No." Kat crossed her arms over her chest. Her eyes swerved from Emily to Penny. "I'm not leaving."

"Get out of here now," Penny hissed, moving toward Kat.

"Make me."

Penny's hand shot out, knocking Kat against the sink counter, her head hitting the mirror. Kat's cry of pain filled the space.

Penny moved cat-like toward Emily. "You and I are leaving here together. You make a sound and I'll show you which knife I brought from Gus's kitchen. Understand?"

Penny slapped Emily's face, knocking her sideways. Pain blossomed in her head. Light flashed behind her eyes. Emily fought to contain the terror whiplashing through her mind as pain shot through her jaw. She felt the pen in her hand. Squeezing her fist tight, leaning toward the woman, she rammed the pen into Penny's side.

"What!" Penny's eyes widened. "You think you can hurt me." Penny grabbed Emily's throat, her fingers tightening. "You're gonna wish you were dead--"

"Take that!" Kat hollered.

Penny grunted. She let go of Emily, pain and shock evident on her face.

"And that!" Kat kicked again and again.

Penny turned, grabbed for Kat.

Emily jabbed the pen into Penny's shoulder. Releasing all the pent up rage and anger she'd felt for this woman she swung her purse hard against the back of Penny's head.

Penny fell, her head connecting with the counter, making a sound like a pumpkin hitting the floor. Emily and Kat watched in disbelieve, their breath coming in huge gasps.

"Did we do that?" Emily asked.

"Is she down for the count?" Kat asked.

"I hope so," Emily replied, hugging Kat. "You must have kicked her hard."

"I did. I was so mad at her for hurting you. And look at you, taking a jab, landing a good hit to her head." Kat looked down at the woman lying on her side, half under the counter. "Do you suppose we knocked her out?"

"No idea." Emily angled around the woman's body, reaching for her wrist.

"What are you doing?" Kat asked.

"Checking for a pulse." The skin beneath her fingers gave off a solid, regular beat. "We'll have to tell them at the desk that someone fainted in the bathroom, I guess," Emily said.

Kat hooted with laughter. "Fainted? Will anyone believe us? Especially when she comes to and starts screaming?"

Emily looked at Kat, realizing that she'd never felt better in her whole life. Whether it was simply the shock of the past few minutes or something else; she was fighting back and she loved it. But she wouldn't admit that to a living soul. Right now, she had more important things to do. "We'll go to the desk and tell them we found her here. After we make sure that Gus isn't going to try anything."

"We'll pretend we know nothing about this woman while we ask about this Gus person?"

"Don't see why not," Emily said. "And by the way, I think it might be helpful if you pretend to be my daughter should anyone ask. I told the security person that I was meeting someone in here. You can be that someone."

"You lied?"

"I lied. I just hit a woman. And I'm about to accuse a man of murder. And I'd do it again."

Kat's eyes went wide. "Cool."

"Yes. Very cool. Let's go." Emily walked beside her, her knee throbbing as they left the bathroom.

No one outside in the main area seemed to take any notice, and when they did it was a surreptitious glance at Kat. Emily understood why. Not only was the young woman wearing dark clothes, had tattoos and black boots, she was at least a head taller than Emily.

Scanning the room as they moved toward the gate, Emily didn't see anyone who looked like Gus. But that didn't mean he wasn't somewhere in the gate area. She squared her shoulders and forced a smile to her lips. She'd get through this. She had faith in Grace that she would get the police and airport security involved. Her daughter was a force to be reckoned with.

When they got to the desk, Emily spoke quietly to the agent, explaining her situation.

"Emily Carling. Yes. We have you on the passenger list," she said, her eyes swerving to Kat and back to Emily.

"This young woman is with me. I'm in danger. There's a man following me. He was behind me in the line going through security. He killed someone. His wife is in the bathroom. She attacked me." Suddenly her mind leaped back to the moment when the video showed Annabelle being strangled. She sobbed. "He's after me. You have to help me."

"Ma'am. There's no one following you."

"There is! Gus Parsons and Penny want to kill me."

"Ma'am, you're upset. I understand you're afraid."

"I'm telling you she's in the bathroom and he's here somewhere. They followed me in here."

"Ma'am, no one will hurt you inside this area. It's secure."

"For Christ's sake! Listen to her. A man *is* after her. He's a killer! A woman tried to strangle her in the bathroom. Call the police!" Kat said, her voice rising with every word.

"Young lady, that's enough."

"If you won't call them, I will." Kat pulled her phone out of her pocket.

"Wait just a minute," the agent said. "Calm down. Both of you."

"Look, my daughter Grace Carling, called the police in St.

John's to report what's happening. Have you not heard anything from her?"

The woman seemed fixated on the tiny chain dangling from Kat's chin. "No, ma'am."

"Give me your phone, Kat. I'm going to call Grace." Quickly, she dialed the number and waited.

"Mom. Where are you?"

"I'm at the gate. But the agent doesn't believe me about Gus."

"Put her on," Grace said, her tone grim.

Emily passed the phone over and watched as the agent's expression went from defiant to concerned. "His name is Gus Parsons?" she asked, staring at Grace.

Grace nodded.

"The police are on their way?" the agent asked.

There was a pause while the agent's expression went from mild interest to outright concern. "She's with your mom. Yes. She did mention that your mom needed help, but I didn't have a name. I'll look after everything. You don't have to worry. Your mother will be safe."

Emily watched as the agent continued to nod and listen. She knew very well what sort of lecture the woman was getting. What sort of not so casual threats her daughter would be making. For the first time in her life, she was elated that her daughter was just like her father.

"Yes," the agent mumbled, the belligerence gone from her voice.

Passing the phone back to Kat, the agent clicked a few keys, picked up the phone and called a number. A few minutes later, a man appeared at her side. He was square set with narrow eyes, and a moustache.

"Mrs. Carling? I'm Mr. Watts, the airport manager." He moved closer. "The police are on their way. We have Mr.

Parsons in my office, but he's claiming you stole from him and are trying to get away. He wants you arrested."

"What! You don't believe him, do you?"

"It doesn't matter what I believe. He's made an accusation and the police have to follow up on it. Please come with me," he said, pointing toward a side door off the gate area.

"No. I'm not going with you. This is insane. Gus Parsons is a killer. He killed his wife, Annabelle. He and Penny, who pretends to be his daughter but is really his wife, killed her together. It's on video," she said, her voice shrill in her ears.

"What?" Mr. Watts said.

Kat stared at her. "Are you sure?"

Emily glanced from Kat to the man who'd made such a ridiculous accusation and realized with a sinking feeling that her story sounded too crazy to be believed: Which meant that in their eyes she was the crazy, perhaps dangerous one. "I'm absolutely certain. I saw the video on his computer of the woman being smothered."

She glanced around the group, to realize that they were staring harder at her. "You've got to believe me."

"Mrs. Carling, you really need to come with me. We'll get this all straightened out when the police get here," Mr. Watts said.

"No. I want to speak to my daughter," she said, holding out her hand to Kat again, who passed her the phone, her brown eyes big as dish plates.

Emily dialed the number, her body trembling with shock. "Grace, there's a man here who needs to speak to you."

"Mom, what does he want?"

"He doesn't believe me about Gus. He thinks I'm crazy."

"I didn't say that, Mrs. Carling," Mr. Watts said, a warning tone in his voice.

"They don't believe what I saw at the house. Gus is accusing me of stealing from him."

"Mom, did you manage to get anything out of the house before you ran?"

"No. My purse. That's it. Nothing else. I was terrified. All I could think about was getting away from there."

"Okay. You have your passport."

"Yes. I never took it out of my purse."

"Put the man on the phone," Grace said, her voice tight.

Emily passed the phone to Mr. Watts. He listened, his eyes flitting from her to the wall behind her, to the agent beside him and back again. "Ms. Carling. I understand your concern for your mother. But she's been accused of stealing."

"I've never stolen anything in my life!" Emily yelled.

"Yes, I'll pass the phone back to your mother."

"Mom, put the phone on speaker. I want to hear what's being said. They can't hold you unless you have something on you that you stole."

"I have the clothes on my back and my purse. That's it. I'm terrified that Gus is going to get in here and take me. They think I'm crazy, but they didn't see what I saw. They didn't hear Penny screaming that she'd kill him if he slept with me. And him swearing that he'd strangle her."

"Mrs. Carling, please calm down," Harry Watts said.

"Not until I get on that plane. You can't keep me here. You have nothing to prove I did anything wrong."

A police officer appeared through the door behind the desk. "Hi Harry, what's going on?"

Harry began to speak. Emily held the phone closer to him. When the officer gave her a quizzical look, she explained, "My lawyer's on the phone and she's asked to hear what you're saying about me."

"Okay. Let's go to your office," the officer said.

"No. I don't want to go there. I'm afraid of him. He's killed other women. He plans to kill me. I came here with nothing but my purse. Not even my luggage. I am afraid for my life. You have to help me."

Her words were met with a stony silence. She tried again.

"Look, I realize that I sound a little crazy, but I'm not. I'm a very sane, capable woman who was conned into coming here by a man who has killed other women. If you don't believe me, go to his house and see. He has an office downstairs where he tracks everything going on around his property. He has videos of everything. One of them shows his wife Annabelle being smothered by Penny." She stopped short, realizing that if she tried to explain Penny's relationship with Gus, they'd be convinced she was crazy.

"He put some sort of bug on my phone and I threw it out back on the highway when he tried to get me to come back. If he gets his hands on me, he'll kill me too. When I ran for my life, he and Penny were in a horrible fight. They were threatening to kill each other." She managed to finish the sentence without sobbing, but her stomach rolled dangerously. She couldn't be sick, not in front of these people who didn't believe her. If she had to go to the bathroom she wasn't sure she'd get out of there without being taken away by the police. At least here at the gate there were other witnesses.

"Those are serious accusations against a member of the community," the police officer said.

"And I could have died, if I hadn't gotten away. Check his house," she said, pushing the words at him as she fought a wave of nausea.

"Officer, that's why I called you hours ago. Where have you been? My mother's in real danger. I insist you check out what my mother is saying," Grace yelled through the phone.

The officer sighed. "Okay. You stay here inside the gate area. Mr. Parsons is with the other officer. I'll go to the house."

. . .

What seemed like hours later, during which Penny was escorted from the bathroom and taken to another office in the building, Emily felt a wall exhaustion hovering around her. She didn't know how much more she could endure. She prayed it would be over soon, and she and Kat would be on their way home.

With the flight for Montreal in its final boarding phase, the phone at the desk rang. The agent answered, a look of disbelief forming on her face.

"Certainly," she said, passing the phone to the airport manager who, by this time, sat slumped in a chair he'd pulled up behind the desk, a weary expression on his face.

"Yes. What did you find?" he said, his voice showing little enthusiasm. Slowly, the man's face went from bored, to blanched, to hollowed out, all in a matter of minutes. "Oh, my God. You're serious?"

He nodded, his eyes flitting around the room, coming to rest on the edge of the desk, a space he now studied with intense interest.

"What do ya think's going on?" Kat whispered.

"Hopefully they found the video." She turned to Kat. "You need to get on the plane. They just gave last call. Everyone else is on board. You don't want to miss it."

"Hey. This is the craziest thing that's ever happened to me. I'm not going anywhere. I'm staying right here with you. Besides, you may need me to defend you," she said, grinning as she applied yet another coat of black lipstick. "By the way, I powered up my phone from my battery pack, if you want to call Grace again."

"Let's wait to see what he says when he gets done looking like death warmed over," Emily said, suddenly feeling a level of elation. For no reason other than the now-engaged look on the man's face. "They must have found something."

He put the phone down. His shoulders slumped. "Ma'am, you're free to go. But we need your contact information."

"Did they find something?" Emily asked.

"The police asked me not to say anything, only that you can go."

"I need to call Grace." She took the phone from Kat's outstretched arm and dialed the number. Grace answered before it stopped ringing. "Mom! Are they holding you? They can't do that. The police have no reason."

"They're not holding me. I can leave. It's been a long day already. Can't wait to see you."

"Me too, Mom," Grace said, her voice thick.

"Love you, darling. See you in a few hours."

"Ma'am," the agent said, "you need to board now."

Emily smiled; the tension knotting her shoulders eased. "We're ready to go."

"I've put this young lady next to you in first class. Compliments of the airline."

"Thank you." With relief sweeping through her, Emily grabbed Kat's arm. "Are you ready?"

"Yes!"

They headed along the ramp leading to the aircraft. "Are you going on from Montreal?" Emily asked, her heart beating a calmer rhythm with her feeling of happiness.

"My mom lives in Montreal with her boyfriend. She said she'll meet me at the airport. Can't wait to tell her all about this. She thinks I'm just a spoiled teenager, but I'm more than that," she said.

"You certainly are."

Fifteen minutes later the plane lifted off the runway. Emily took a deep cleansing breath.

It was over. All over.

EPILOGUE

Three months later:

"Mom, the phone's for you," Grace said, as she came into the kitchen.

She and Grace had been busy all morning with the stager. Emily was selling her house. It wasn't that she didn't love the place, but her life had changed so much in recent months. After she got home to Boston, and for weeks after that, she could hardly believe what she'd lived through, the days she spent not knowing that the man she believed she loved planned to kill her.

Once back in Boston, she'd been interviewed by a member of the Royal Canadian Mounted Police around everything that she'd seen and heard and experienced during her relationship with Gus Parsons. She'd signed affidavits and written statements...

When she was told they found Millie Hansen's body buried in a shallow grave near Gros Morne park, Grace could hardly believe that her friend had fallen prey to those two killers as well. Having seen the video of Annabelle, it broke her heart to think about how her friend must have died in the same horrible circumstances.

The police had treated Gus's home, Penny's condo, and their vehicles as crime scenes. It turned out that Penny and Gus met while working at a psychiatric hospital in British Columbia where she worked as a ward secretary and he as an orderly. Together they'd stolen the identity of a derelict who had been a patient at the hospital.

The police confirmed that Penny was his wife, and that Tessa was the daughter. Although Gus has been uncooperative, Penny's anger issues led her to disclose that the killings in St. John's weren't the only ones. Because of her they were investigating unsolved murders in Kingston and Barrie, looking for similarities in contacts and locations. They were also checking into the hospital in British Columbia to see if they could find out more about the two killers, especially where they lived before they came to Ontario.

A search of his property in St. John's found two bodies, one identified as Louise Sanderson. Because Annabelle's death had been considered to be from natural causes, Gus as her husband had been able to have her body cremated, leaving them with only the evidence on the tape. But it was enough to charge Gus and Penny with murder, and almost certainly there would be more charges to follow as soon as all the evidence was collected.

The officer thanked her again for all her help, saying how brave she was to get out before she was killed. She didn't feel brave. She didn't feel safe. Late at night, she wondered if she'd ever feel safe again.

After the intense questioning by the police in the weeks after she got back to Boston, she couldn't handle anything, at least it felt that way. Everything seemed like such an effort for her. She'd been in counseling since she got home, due to the terrifying experiences she'd endured and the nightmares that still haunted her.

"Thanks, Grace." She put the phone to her ear. "Hello."

"Mrs. Carling. It's Officer Longstaff from the RCMP in St. John's. I promised to get back in touch when I knew more. Have you got a minute?"

"Certainly."

"There's going to be a press conference this afternoon, but I wanted to give you a heads up ahead of time. As you know we were in the midst of a very labor-intensive search for other victims when Penny learned that Gus had murdered two other women and buried them on his property.

When we gave her that information she turned on him and provided us with all kinds of information about their activities in the last twenty years. In addition to the deaths and bodies she told us about we are checking all other possible leads around deaths across Canada of women who fit the description: vulnerable, living alone, with limited social contacts. We know that each murder was committed using different techniques, making it difficult to develop a pattern. Each was unique. But with you and Millie Hansen he upped the game, using online dating sites to groom his victims."

"How many others?" she asked, afraid to know, but unable to resist asking.

"I can't confirm a number at the moment as it's an ongoing investigation. I wanted you to hear from me about what we're looking at here, and to tell you that you're a very lucky woman. We found two bodies in what you thought was a pet cemetery. Two women he'd gotten from the women's shelter where he was a board member. Easy access to vulnerable women seemed to be the key to those two killings."

"That's horrible!" Emily shivered at the memory of the

scarf and what had to have been blood stains. "No wonder Gus nearly had a heart attack when I found that scarf."

"Yes, the scarf will be very useful in identifying the second victim found in the garden."

"What about Tessa?"

"She's will be looked after by child services here in St. John's."

"So sad," Emily said, remembering the little girl's sweet smile.

"Are you doing okay?" he asked.

"Not bad. My daughter has been such a help. I've been in contact with Millie's family. It's awful."

"By way of a reminder, this is still an ongoing investigation, and if you remember anything else please call me. In the meantime, take care." He hung up, leaving Emily feeling desolate and just a little afraid despite being safely back in Boston. Yet she was so relieved that the investigation was continuing.

"That was the police." She explained to Grace what the officer had told her.

"We're going to watch the news on CBC this evening. I want to know what's going on. After what you went through and the deaths of those women, I hope Gus Parsons goes to prison for the rest of his life."

"I hope so, too," Emily said, her thoughts on Tessa.

Later that evening, they found the CBC news online and watched as the police gave information on the three deaths in St. John's, four in Ontario, and five suspected cases in British Columbia and Alberta being investigated as deaths possibly related to the husband and wife team of serial killers.

"This is the first time that crimes reflecting such callous

indifference and cold-blooded murder across the entire country are being investigated," Officer Longstaff said in conclusion. "Now I'd like to introduce the criminologist who has been leading our investigation being carried out across the country. Pat Bonnell."

A woman stepped up to the podium, her serious expression was made even more somber by her black suit and black hair pulled back in a severe bun at the nape of her neck, and black framed glasses. "Thank you," she said, as she turned to face the cameras. "What I'd like to talk about here is something that the public should be aware of in this modern age of online dating. The last woman who nearly ended up being his next victim had been lured by him through a dating site for seniors."

The reporters started asking questions, drowning one another out.

"I don't want to go into the particulars at this time. I simply want to warn women out there who are connecting with men on these dating sites, or any site that offers a connection or the chance for a relationship. Please be very careful. Many of the participants on these sites are looking to con their victims into giving them money, sometimes their entire life savings. It's a growing threat in today's world, one that we all must take seriously, especially all of you out there who are considering these sites as a possible place to connect with someone."

Pat Bonnell shifted her weight from one foot to the other, her expression becoming even more intense and stern. "But Gus Parsons's plan was different, worse than just conning money from his victims. He wanted the money, but he also went on the site with the intention of luring women to their deaths."

She adjusted her glasses and continued. "He portrayed himself as every woman's dream. His behavior online was perfectly normal, engaging and charming, nothing that would alert the potential victim to his behavior. He gained their trust by being everything they wanted in a man; caring, concerned and professing to be madly in love. After getting to know them online, he played on their feelings, created an imaginary life where they'd be together, that the woman would have a wonderful, adoring partner for life."

"Until recently, he had lured women through contacts he and his wife developed within the community wherever they lived. But then he found the Internet dating sites that offered easy and vulnerable victims. In recent months he and his wife got their first victim from an online dating sight. A woman who believed him, who trusted him, and had been lured to her death. And if it hadn't been for another woman's luck and her ability to think quickly, he would have gotten his second victim using his online profile."

"Mom, I'm turning this off. We don't need to hear any more."

After the screen went dark Emily sat there, the full realization of her peril, sinking in at the woman's words. "She's right. He was every woman's dream. He was my dream. I was hours away from dying. How many other women like me are out there? Dreaming of a life with what seems like a perfectly wonderful man. I wish I could find a way to help them not make the mistake I did."

"Mom, you can't save the world, and you can't save women bent on hooking up with these men. Look at how hard I tried to convince you not to go."

"I know. But you see, that's the issue. These women need to talk with someone who's been victimized by this type of man. I could help. I could share how I felt, how much I believed in his story because he said all the right things. He behaved as if he really cared, when all the time he planned to kill me."

"Mom. You're not going anywhere or doing anything. We're selling your house, getting you into a secure condo. And we're going to put all of this behind us."

She looked at Grace, at her daughter who never in her life backed down from a fight; choosing a career to match her talents.

Emily wished she could be more like her daughter, but that was life. Everyone has to find their way. And maybe she'd find her way to help these women who were desperate to find love in their later years. Putting themselves in peril.

She decided right then and there, that if she should find such an organization that could help these people, she would become involved. She'd take a page from her daughter's book and learn not to back down, not to be a victim.

She reached out and took her daughter's hand in hers. "I'm sorry I made you worry."

Grace leaned over and kissed her cheek. "You did, but it's all over now. Completely over."

THE END

≈

Dear Reader,

I am so pleased you read Falling Prey, the fourth book in my Women in Danger series. If you don't mind, would you consider reviewing Falling Prey on AMAZON? Thank you.

The Women in Danger series includes three other books, one of which I am featuring here.

Desperate Memories is a story of a woman who is being hunted by a man from her past who will kill her if she can't determine who he is.

Here's an excerpt from Desperate Memories.

~

The snap of gunfire cut the air. Robyn McGill leapt back, slamming her shoulder into the stern rail of the sailboat. Fear choked the breath from her lungs as she slid into the safety of the cockpit.

Her movements were slowed by a sense of disbelief as she edged along the roughened, fiberglass decking. With the light of the companionway guiding her, she crawled toward the safety of the cabin until her fingers bumped against cold metal. She gripped the rounded, deadly shape of a gun.

Panic pulsed through her, as if driven by a giant bellows, penetrating every part of her being. This couldn't be happening to her. Not here. Not now.

She sensed a sudden movement near the bow of the boat.

"Nathan? Peter?" Robyn's words joined the gray mist floating around her as she grabbed the boat's wheel and pulled herself to her feet.

Her eyes scanned the forward deck. The only sound was the lap, lap, lap of the frigid Atlantic water against the hull, and the occasional slap of a sail in the fog-shrouded stillness. Silence, like a malevolent force, clung to everything.

She needed to talk to Nathan, to feel her fiancé's arms around her, to be reassured she had only dreamed––

There! Another movement beyond the cabin door near the foresail. "Nathan," she cried, her breath leaving a trail of mist in the cool night air.

Silence.

Terror stiffened her shoulders, making her heart smash into her ribs.

Robyn slid down the companionway to the cabin below. Her gaze swept the space. Gleaming teak and the smooth, rounded surfaces of the cabin's interior were awash in the muted light offered by brass sconces.

In the comfort of the luxurious quarters below deck, Robyn could almost believe that nothing was wrong. She walked toward the bow of the boat, checking each space as she went: the head, silent and immaculate; the mirrored hanging locker, displaying a full-length image of a woman whose eyes radiated fear as they peered back at her. And finally, the forward cabin with its rich, burgundy duvet and shimmering brass lamps.

A silver framed photo of her brother, Peter, holding a prized racing trophy was displayed in a stationary frame attached to the table. His insulated storm jacket lay on the bed next to his wallet and keys. Everything was just as it should be. Robyn sobbed in relief.

She knew where the men in her life were and what they were doing: playing cards in the cabin at the stern of the boat. She raced back, through the main cabin, and flung open the door to the aft suite. "You guys had me scared to death!"

Her hands clutched the door. The graphic violence of the room yanked the air from her lungs. Pictures dangled crookedly from the walls. The locker door clung to the wall by a single hinge. The mattress of the queen-sized bed lay disemboweled, bleeding white foam through huge tears in the quilted fabric.

"Oh, My God!" Robyn sobbed as she covered her mouth to block a scream, her fingers cold and sticky against her lips.

Slowly, she lifted her hands from her face. Half-dried blood covered her palms and traced bizarre patterns up the length of her quivering fingers.

A bloodcurdling scream tore from her lips.

The ringing of a phone filled the air, wrenching her awake and away from the painful nightmare. Force of habit had Robyn clutching the phone before it stopped ringing. "Yes."

"Dr. McGill?"

"Yes."

"It's the Emergency Room calling. There's been a six-car pileup, and we need all the help we can get."

Robyn groped in the darkness for the bedside lamp and turned it on, flooding the room with light. "I'll be right there," she muttered while a ghostlike dream faded into the night.

Dropping the phone back into its cradle, she slumped against the pillows. Try as she might, she couldn't bring the dream back from its hiding place. All that remained was an overwhelming sense of guilt that she was somehow responsible for what happened. A guilt that years of therapy could not erase.

What had she done that was so awful as to cause this recurring nightmare? It had to have some basis in reality. She'd awakened the same way for the past two nights, to the same nightmare that had plagued her for three years.

Was it only a disturbing nightmare? Born of her imagination and all her unanswered questions? A terrible dream of no real importance, with no basis in reality?

Robyn hoped so, but didn't know anymore.

She threw back the bedclothes and scuffed down the hall to the bathroom. Not wanting to wake her ten-year-old nephew, Jason, who slept soundly in his room, Robyn eased the door closed and turned on the light.

Her eyes ached as light flooded over her. Squinting into the mirror, she rubbed a damp facecloth over her heated skin. Worry lines marred her expression, making the anxiety in her eyes stand out against her pallid skin.

Once again she was gripped by an unsettling sense of foreboding. While she waited for the confusing feelings to fade away as they always did, she shoved her tear-matted hair from her forehead and wished with all her heart that the nightmare would just go away. And stay away.

Her fingers trembled against her pale lips. Her throat

ached, her head pounded in rhythm with her heart. More than anything in the world, Robyn prayed she'd feel safe again.

Maybe it was too late.

Maybe it had always been too late...

You can purchase Desperate Memories on AMAZON

ABOUT THE AUTHOR

Stella MacLean is a story teller. Simple as that.

An author of books, both fiction and nonfiction, she has served as Writer in Residence at Vancouver Public Library in Vancouver, British Columbia. She loves to travel, spend time with friends and family, along with her husband and her fur babies in her home near the Bay of Fundy in Atlantic Canada.

Stella relishes the hours she spends hiding out in her office making up stories about the lives of imaginary people. Having found love again in the third act of her life, Stella enjoys telling stories about people who find love elusive and complicated, but still try with all their hearts.

Stella's past includes being a registered nurse, from which she has drawn story ideas for several of her books. She went back to university when her children were older and was granted a Commerce Degree, majoring in Accounting, from Mount Allison University in Sackville, New Brunswick, Canada.

OTHER BOOKS BY STELLA MACLEAN

THE RIGHT GUY SERIES

Finding Mr. Wrong

Finding Mr. Gorgeous

Finding Mr. Valentine

Finding Mr. Fixit

Finding Mr. Amazing

LOVE ALWAYS SERIES

Remembering You

The Good Daughter

LOVE IS ETERNAL

Young Love

Of Love and Life

WOMEN IN DANGER

Unimaginable

Desperate Memories

Desperate Acts

Falling Prey

HARLEQUIN BOOKS

Unexpected Attraction

Bringing Emma Home

NON-FICTION

Living Successfully With Chronic Pain

www.ingramcontent.com/pod-product-compliance
Lightning Source LLC
Chambersburg PA
CBHW020630180626
46816CB00003B/892